THE IRON DOOR INN MYSTERIES

By A. C. Boyan

Contents

This is a work of fiction. Names, characters, places, and incidents either are the product of the author's imagination or are used fictitiously, and any resemblance to actual persons, living or dead, is entirely coincidental.

ISBN 0-9671795-1-3

Front and back cover designs and photographs

A. C. Boyan

THE IRON DOOR INN MYSTERIES

HOW LUCKY CAN YOU GET?

By A. C. Boyan

"Charles will you stop somewhere before we get to the Inn. We need some sunscreen and trail mix."

"I need gas, too."

Charles and Doris Knowles live in Seattle, Washington and were on their way to the Iron Door Inn. They had stayed there on previous occasions and received a letter from Harry Wright, the owner, stating that he had made the decision to market the Inn. He explained that, since they were coming for another visit and had shown a previous interest, he would hold off doing so until they arrived.

Charles and Doris were retired: he from teaching criminal psychology at the University of Washington and she from different jobs working in the hospital, library, being a housewife, and volunteering. Doris had neat white hair and a pleasant face that always seem to have a little smile.

"Did he mention why he's selling the Inn?" Doris asked.

"Not in the letter. He just said he was over extended and asked if I wanted to invest some money in the Inn I told him I wanted to retire to southern Arizona; you said it was your favorite Inn. Maybe he thought you wanted it."

"That's right. We were all sitting on the patio watching that beautiful sunset, but I wasn't thinking about buying an Inn."

Charles filled his tank and went in to the Circle K. Doris handed him some items and continued to look around. He stood in line to pay for the gas and items and overheard the man in front of him say to the clerk. "Only a million this week? Wasn't it ten million last week?"

"Yeah, some guy in Tucson won it."

"How lucky can you get? I'll settle for a million. Give me two quick picks," the man said.

Charles thought a million would go a long way in providing a carefree retirement. He wasn't a gambler, knowing the odds, but on occasion he would buy a ticket so he said to the clerk, "Add a quick pick."

In the car Doris said, "I heard you ask for a quick pick, what's that?'

"A lottery ticket. Winning that would buy us an Inn."

Doris gave him a narrow glance and said, "I am not getting too excited over that, fat chance. What number did you play?"

"I don't know."

Doris, eyes wide, looked puzzled and repeated, "You don't know? Then how did you get a number?"

"I got a Quick Pick. Computer picks for you."

"I think I would rather pick my own number. That would be more fun."

"If we did win, would you be interested in buying the Inn?"

"It is beautiful." Doris looked out at the roadside wild flowers and the mountains in the distance. "It might be hard work."

"It'll be interesting to talk to Harry about it. If we won the lottery we wouldn't have to worry about running it."

On the patio of the Iron Door Inn the proprietor's, Harry and Lisa Wright, enjoyed their late lunch and the view of the Santa Catalina Mountains. The Inn was located in the foothills of the mountains on an old route that ran north from Tucson to Globe. Today a modern road paralleled the old route making the Inn accessible, but still isolated. It was surrounded by State and

National Park land, insuring the pristine beauty of the area.

"Do you remember Charles and Doris Knowles?

"Bird watchers. Sweet lady. I remember how excited they got seeing the Roadrunner with a snake in its beak down by the wash. Why do you ask?"

"They're coming for another visit and I'm going to ask them if they'd be interested in buying or investing in the place."

"You're what? What the hell are you talking about? We don't need any partners and I am not going to sell the place. Are we in trouble again?"

"Well, we are overextended a bit, and I don't like it here anymore–too much work and very little profit."

A shadow of sadness spread across Lisa's pretty face. "Are you gambling again? I thought we left that behind. Damn Harry, that's my inheritance invested in this Inn and what do you care about the work? I do most of it and I love it. We've been here four years, I never heard you say you were unhappy. I think you're lying Harry. This is our last chance Harry, my inheritance saved us the last time, if we lose this, then we won't have money to start over. You better make it work. The next time you get any bright ideas you better talk to the senior partner first."

Lisa was a thirty-two-year-old bright, hardworking woman and her past experiences with Harry had toughened her, but it was not innate in her personality, it was just a survival tool that she used when necessary.

Harry was about six foot, heavy around the middle with receding thin light brown hair and was a couple of years older than Lisa. A very exposed and tense looking Harry with his elongated face looking longer, said, "Right, you're right, I suppose we can work something out. I'll talk to them anyway. I'll tell them we haven't completely decided and we're just in the talking stage."

"Do what you have to, but after that you'd better do everything you can to keep us afloat."

The oldest building on the property was called the maintenance building. An Inn had been on this location since 1879. It was a stagecoach stop about twenty miles North of Tucson on a trail connecting Tucson and Globe. Four years ago, the main building was renovated and a new tin roof and four rooms were added to the maintenance building. It had two rooms on each end. The rooms were Spartan and were to be used to accommodate employees. The building was long and wide with the middle used for maintenance equipment and supplies for the Inn. A section of this area had been separated for use as a lunch area for the staff. After having lunch here, two employees, Carlos and Louisa, went back to her room.

Louisa Perez was a friendly girl with dark fine features, long black hair and a small build. After dropping out of high school, her goal was to save up enough money to get her own place and later, with experience, get a better paying job at one of the large resorts. The advantage of her working here was that the owner didn't require a lot experience. Because of the Inn's isolated location–and the fact the owner liked to have some staff available twenty-four hours a day–he rented it to employees for a small fee. It was perfect for Louisa. She would save on rent, car expenses and get experience.

When she met Carlos, who was working there as a grounds keeper and occupying the room next to hers, they became romantically involved. Carlos was a well built, medium height, good looking man a few years older than she. Her plans changed.

Sitting on the bed in the small room she looked painfully up at Carlos. "Carlos we must have enough money to go to California with your cousin by now. How much do we need? I don't like stealing. I'm sorry I ever did it. You said you love me. You don't ask people you love to steal." Tears flowed from her eyes as she looked longingly at Carlos to reply.

When he didn't immediately reply she hysterically said, "I'm afraid of getting caught. What will we do then? I might go to jail. I never should have done this."

Carlos slowly sat on the bed and took her hand. This emotional outburst had been building for six months. With a furrowed brow and deep sigh he said in a controlled tone. "Louisa, Louisa, calm down. If you did what I told you, not to take a lot of money, just small amounts, no credit cards, in rooms you weren't scheduled to clean, chances are they wouldn't miss it. They would think they misplaced it. It's going to be all right. Calm down. When we get to California everything will be all right. There's plenty of work there. We'll live a lot better."

"It'll feel good to get out of the car. I can't wait to walk those canyon trails. I think the last time we were here we added five new birds to our list."

"Don't forget the Mariposa Lily, it was our first sighting, a rare find and so beautiful."

"I love the weather here. It's so warm. I can't wait to change into lighter clothing."

The Inn had large oak doors hung with massive iron hinges. Most people thought this was the derivation of the name. It wasn't, it came from the old Iron Door Mine back in the mountains, not far from here.

Walking through these doors, Charles and Doris entered a large lobby with western decor. A large leather couch and two leather chairs stood in front of the fireplace. The walls were covered with paintings of working cowboys, mountain scenes, and foothills desert vegetation featuring the giant cacti, the saguaro.

A voice from behind the front desk said graciously, "Welcome back Mr. and Mrs. Knowles. It's a pleasure to see you. Did you have a good trip?"

Charles in his distinguished manner said, "Yes it went very well thank you. I think you can call us Charles and Doris, no need to be formal, especially on vacation. Yours is Lisa, right?"

Smiling, Lisa replied, "Yes, completely."

"Completely, oh yes of course, no pun intended." Charles said, flushing with embarrassment under his neatly trimmed white beard.

"It happens with a name like Wright. It's only annoying when it's intentional. Would you like the same room you had on your last visit?"

"I'd love that room," Doris said, "aren't we lucky it's available."

"Then room 16 it is. Enjoy your stay."

Half way across the lobby, Doris said, "I love these vaulted ceilings and large windows."

"Yeah, and the large beams and all the woodwork."

This exchange was interrupted by a man making long strides across the lobby, "I see you made it, good to see you again. How was the trip?"

"Wonderful, it is just like traveling from winter to summer. How are things with you Harry?"

"Our bookings have been good. I think it's directly related to cold winters. When the temperatures in the North go down, our bookings go up. And you, Doris, how are things with you?"

"Fine Harry. The place looks wonderful and we got the same room as on our last visit. I noticed you added flower boxes on the wall surrounding the outside patio. They look great."

"Thank you. That was Lisa's idea. She does have a knack for decorating. Well, I'll let you two settle in and, if it's convenient, perhaps we could have breakfast in the morning. Around eight?"

"That sounds great. We'll be there."

They walked into the room and Doris drew the drapes back exposing the mountain vista. With a sigh she said,

"It's breathtakingly beautiful, I never get tired of it Charles. It inspires me to take up painting."

"You should. You're very artistic.

"Maybe it's my intuition," Doris said, "but their bookings are good, they've made improvements, the place appears to be well maintained, do you think Lisa is as interested in selling as Harry?"

"I don't know. I do know she's responsible for the physical operation. I think he handles the financial end. Could be marital or money problems. Maybe we will find out at breakfast.

Charles stepped out onto the guest filled patio and spotted Harry at a table in the far corner. A recognition smile in that direction was returned with a wave by Harry.

"Another beautiful morning Harry."

"Good morning Charles, Doris, yes it is. What are your plans for today? By the looks of your attire I would guess some hiking."

Doris said, "Yes, in the canyon. Do you know what the wildflower situation is?"

"The guests say it's great. We had good November rain and that triggers a good display of spring wildflowers."

After he said this, Harry motioned to the waitress who briskly moved to the table to take their order.

When she left, Charles said, "Knowing that you and Lisa love the place, I was surprised by your letter.

"We do, but sometimes we go through a stage when we think we might like to try something else. It's not as much work as it was during the startup years, but it is a demanding business. The profit margin so tight you have to keep employees at a minimum and try to do as much as you can yourself.

Doris said, "You have made significant improvements, it would seem the worst is over. I know some friends who do that for a living. They buy a small business, fix it up and sell it for a profit."

The waitress, with a minimum of interruption, placed their orders on the table. "No, nothing like that. Actually, we have reconsidered. It's just a stage you go through. I do think retirement would be nice. Quite naturally I think. How about you, enjoying your retirement?"

Despite his polite demeanor, Charles felt that Harry's eye movements, fidgeting, and change of subject, telegraphed his uneasiness.

"We are," Charles said, "but a change in climate is in order, and this area has that, and is perfect for people who enjoy outdoor activities."

"Do you and Lisa enjoy outdoor activities?" Doris asked.

"Not as much as Lisa. I enjoy the beauty, but I'm not into the physical part of it. I'm not a hiker. What line of work were you in Charles?"

"I was a psychology teacher at the University of Washington."

Doris, not wanting her husband viewed as a sedate college professor said, "He also taught courses on Criminal Psychology and Motivation and was a consultant for the Seattle Police Department."

"Wow! That sounds interesting, but how would you put that knowledge into practice."

Charles now realized they would not be returning to the original subject of the meeting. "It's not so complicated. In cases where the motive is not clear or you can't establish any premeditation, studying the stress level of people connected to the victim will develop good investigative leads. The buildup of stress can lead to the eruption of violence."

"That's pretty heavy stuff, but talking about criminal activity on a smaller scale, I have a situation here that maybe you could help me solve."

"How so?" Charles asked.

"It seems that for the last six weeks there have been small amounts of money missing from guests' rooms. I don't know the extent of it because I don't believe all the cases were reported to us. Perhaps some of guests thought they lost, mislaid, or miscounted their money. In fact, some of the guests reported it as if it were lost hoping it might be found and turned in."

Doris put her coffee cup down and said. "That's not the type of activity that would be good for business, if it were known."

"Certainly not, that's why I have been reluctant to call in the authorities. I think I'll try to solve it myself. Now, to answer your question. Would you be willing to leave some marked bills in your room?"

Charles and Doris looked at each with expressions of agreement. Charles said, "We don't have a problem with that. Glad to help."

"Fine, I'll mark up some bills and bring them around this evening."

Charles and Doris had settled in for the evening. He had a book and she had her needlework. "Charles, what do you call those horses? They were so magnificent."

They're called Tennessee Walking Horses."

"They really surprised me. I was concentrating on that bird and when I turned around there they were on the trail. Were they rented?"

"No. You can rent horses though, there's a stable adjacent to the Catalina State Park entrance. That's the only stable that has a permit to use the park's equestrian trails. The park has a camping area and corrals for people bringing their horses. The man on the first horse explained that that's where they are staying. They came to Tucson to be in the La Fiesta de Los Vaqueros rodeo parade."

A knock on the door drew their attention and Doris opened the door and said, "Good evening Harry come in."

"Evenin', looks like you're relaxing after an adventurous day."

Charles straightened up in his chair, laid down his book and said. "That we are Harry and what a pleasant day it was."

Harry pulled some bills from his pocket. "Here are the bills for the bait. I marked them with luminescent ink. It totals a hundred, three twenties, three tens, and two fives."

Getting up from his chair Charles accepted the bills. "Is there any particular spot or arrangement that they should be in."

"No, just make it look natural. It was interesting that all the other victims mentioned it was when they returned from the pool that they discovered the money missing."

"That's interesting, I think most people do leave their valuables in the room when they go to the pool. It also indicates that the perpetrator could plainly see who was at the pool from most of the rooms." Charles said.

Doris, looking up from her needlework asked, "Are the maids assigned rooms to clean, or do they randomly clean them?"

"The vacant rooms are cleaned in the morning for incoming guests. The occupied rooms are cleaned in the afternoon. The head housekeeper keeps a record of which maid cleaned a room. What are your plans for tomorrow?"

"Doris wants to do some shopping in Tucson in the morning and then I think it will be a relaxing afternoon lounging by the pool."

"That will work. Have a good night and I'll talk to you tomorrow."

Charles picked up his book and looked concerned as he said, "Is this going to distract from your vacation Doris?'

"Oh no Charles, I know it's a hobby with you. If you're comfortable with it, I'm fine. Actually I think it adds a little excitement."

Charles walked over to the dresser, set his book down, and picked up the marked bills. "As an added precaution I think I'll write down the serial numbers on these bills. What I find interesting is that if they know who cleaned the room and the time frame of the theft, it seems unlikely that, if it was that person, they would think they could get away with it."

Carlos sat in his room drinking beer and listening to rap on his CD player. His cell phone rang. "Hey cousin what's up?'

"Everything man, it's going down tomorrow. Can you be ready by six?"

"Yeah, I guess I can. I don't have much to take."

"I 'm not worried about you. You could put your stuff in a pillow case. What about Louisa?"

"I'm not taking Louisa."

"You're not! She's cool man. Why not?"

"She's freaking me out. She can't take the pressure. Last night she went postal."

"What are you going to tell her?"

"Nothing man, nothing, she's filling in for a sick kitchen worker tonight. I just won't see her. That's all. Could I stay with you tonight? It would be better. That way there is no chance I see her tonight."

"Cool man, it's you loss. That will be better. I won't have to worry about you being late. I got some other dudes to pick up in the morning."

"Well Charles, do you think we've been robbed?" Doris said, when they returned from the pool late Saturday afternoon.

Charles transferred the bag and towels they brought to the pool to one arm while he fumbled for the room key.

"There's a possibility, it's been happening for six months."

"It seems like a simple trap, I wonder why he didn't try it before." Doris didn't wait for an answer. "I think the whole idea came to him when we were supposed to be discussing the sale of the Inn. When he heard you did consulting for the police it became a good diversion. It helped him change the subject and also solve his problem. One which wouldn't surprise me if Lisa hadn't been after him to solve."

Charles placed the bag and towels on the bed and went over to the dresser. There, spread out on the top was the contents of his pockets including the marked bills. He counted the bills and turned toward Doris. "Sixty dollars, sixty dollars missing."

"Are you sure? Let's look on the floor around the dresser, maybe it fell while the maid was cleaning."

"Yeah, fell into her pocket. You're right though. Let's check all the possibilities before we call Harry."

After Charles called Harry, he said, "He wants us to stop by his office on the way to dinner."

Doris was working on her nails. She looked up and asked, "What was his reaction?"

"He was surprised just like us."

Lisa and Harry both had offices. Hers was adjacent to the front desk where she could keep a close watch on the operation. It was a working office and had a warm feminine touch to it. Pictures on the desk and wall and fresh flowers on the desk.

Harry's was down the hall, more private, and nearer to the north side exit of the Inn. It had older, more traditional wooden furniture; a computer, safe and filing cabinets. The general lighting of the room was dark, with the exception of the halogen lamp on the desk.

"Had a visit from the Knowles? Lisa said as she entered the office. "I just passed them in the hall."

"Yes, I asked them to help me set a trap for our in house thief."

"I am glad you're addressing the problem, but do you think it's a good idea to involve guests. It's not a good idea to broadcast we have a thief working here."

"True, but in this case the guest has worked for the police and I'm sure he is discreet."

"Really, professional help. You were reluctant to bring in the police. Have a change of heart?"

Harry playing with a pencil answered. "This is different. I'll call in the police when I have more evidence and I might be close to that now. Can you tell me who cleaned Room 16 today?" Did you bring the sign off sheet?"

"Yes." Lisa looked at the list and said, "It was Maria. That's strange because I saw Louisa coming out of that room and she didn't sign off, Maria did."

"That's logical because a thief would not want to be connected to the crime. I'll question Louisa."

Nodding her head Lisa asked, "That's very good Harry, but how do you propose to connect the thief to the crime?"

"I marked the bills with luminescent ink. This UV penlight will show the marking."

Looking doubtful Lisa said, "Do you think she's going to cooperate?"

"We'll see. I'm going to give her a choice, she will let me, or the police check her bills."

"I hope it works. At least you're doing something."

That evening about 8:30 PM a loud howling sound startled Maria. It wasn't so much the sound, for it was a common one, but it was close and more than two. The sound of a pack of coyotes. Maria went to the window and looked out. She didn't see the coyotes; she saw a dark figure heading to the side entrance to the Inn.

Sunday morning the mist was lifting and swirling around the mountains. Seated at a table on the flagstone patio waiting for breakfast, Charles and Doris were enjoying the view.

"Doris, when I'm vacationing I have a wonderful appetite. It must be the fresh air or the exercise."

Although Charles was trim and in good physical condition, Doris tried to help him chose healthy foods. "Perhaps it's not eating all those snacks between meals."

"Could be. My eating is much more disciplined here."

"Did we win the lottery? Shopping yesterday I saw so many nice things I'd like to buy."

"Oh, right. I'll have to check the paper." Searching in his pockets for the ticket, he came out empty handed and said, "It must be in the room somewhere."

Lisa walked up to the table and said, "Good morning, may I join you."

"Of course." Doris said.

Lisa sat down and addressed the waitress who had just placed their meals on the table. "Anna would you bring me coffee and a croissant?" To Anna's acknowledgment she said, "Thank you." Turning her attention back to Charles and Doris she said, "I understand Harry has recruited you to help solve the Iron Door Inn caper."

Charles smiled and said. "Yes, we've signed on."

At that moment Harry joined the party. Anna walked over and asked, "Would you like breakfast Mr. Wright?"

"No thank you Anna I've had breakfast. A coffee will be fine."

Lisa perked up and asked. "How did your investigation go?'

"Uneventful. I didn't find anything."

Not satisfied with this abrupt answer Lisa probed on. "Did she cooperate? Was she embarrassed? What was her reaction?"

"No, she was calm. I told her the situation and that she would probably be more comfortable with me than the police."

This struck a chord with Doris who said. "That seems unusual. A young girl being questioned about a theft, I would expect her to be nervous. I know I would."

Moving his plate away, Charles put his forearms on the table and leaned forward. "Did you scan any bills with the penlight?"

"Yes, she cooperated and emptied her purse. She took out the bills from her wallet and handed them to me. She also said I could look anywhere in the room I wanted."

Lisa motioned to Anna to bring more coffee. "Did you check Maria and Tina after that?"

Harry gave a hesitated reply brought on by surprise, "No I didn't. Louisa probably had it. I just couldn't find it."

Charles sat back in his chair and thought that was a premature end to the investigation. Charles had made a career of studying human nature and knew it was complex. To him, this was just another enigma to think about.

"Mrs. Wright, excuse me."

Lisa looked up at a very emotional Maria. "Yes, Maria what is it?"

"I'm sorry to bother you, but I am worried about Louisa, she didn't show up for work. I went to check on her. I pounded on her door. She didn't answer. So, I checked Carlos' room and he didn't answer. I went back and looked in Maria's window. Oh GOD! She was on the bed and she didn't look right. Oh GOD! I'm frightened."

The normal din of the guests on the patio became subdued. All the guests were focused on Maria. All four at the table rose simultaneously and Lisa put her arm around Maria. "It'll be all right Maria. She's probably sick. We'll go check."

Harry and Charles headed toward Louisa's room with the others following.

Harry and Charles arrived on the scene first and stood on the porch in front of Louisa's door. The porch ran the width of the building and both Carlos' and Louisa's rooms opened onto it. Harry unlocked the door and pushed it open slowly and called out her name. "Louisa, Louisa. Oh my GOD! Oh my GOD! What's happened?"

Charles, who had experience with gruesome sights, working with the police, was still deeply moved by young Louisa's body sprawled on the bed. He heard voices outside. "Don't let them come in Harry. I'll check the body. Have someone call 911."

"I'll tell them." Harry stepped onto the porch and raised his hands in a stopping position. "Don't go in. Lisa call 911."

"What has happened to Louisa? It can't be! My GOD she's dead." Maria let out a sorrowful scream that only comes from the piercing of the soul. With this came an emotional breakdown.

Lisa and Doris with astounded looks of disbelief both took hold of Maria. Doris, with tears welling in her eyes, said, "Lisa, you go call 911 and I'll take Maria back to the Inn."

Charles stepped out on the porch, closed the door and said in a low voice. "She's dead Harry."

"What do we do? GOD this is awful. I don't even know if she has relatives. The closest one to her was Carlos and he's gone."

"We wait for the police. I'll stay here and you go back and stay with the ladies. I think they will need some support."

Charles's career had steeled his external reactions but nothing could buffer the deep sadness he felt from seeing the body of a young girl brutally slain. He had lectured on criminal psychology at the university, at seminars for law enforcement agencies and written a book on the subject, but in the end the question of how any human being could do that to another goes unanswered. His thoughts were interrupted by the arrival of the emergency vehicle as it stopped in front of the building.

Charles stood up and pointed to the room as two members of the EMT unit, carrying their equipment, moved quickly into the room. In a couple of minutes three more vehicles pulled up and raised a cloud of dust. One was the scene of the crime unit and the other two were squads. It was like the changing of the guard. The EMT people came out and the crime scene unit took over. Two uniformed officers and one in plain clothes went into the room and in a few minutes the plain clothes one came out and addressed himself to Charles.

He was medium height and well-built and wearing a starched white shirt with sharply creased black pants. "I'm Manny Gomez, a detective with the Pima County Sheriff's Department."

"I'm Charles Knowles, a guest here.'

"Did you discover the body?"

"Yes, but we were alerted to the problem by a girl named Maria."

"You said we. Who were the others?"

The answer was postponed by Harry's arrival on the scene. Reacting to this, Charles said, "This is Harry Wright. Lisa and Harry own the Inn. Harry, this is Detective Manny Gomez of the Pima County Sheriff's Department."

Harry, reaching up and running his hand through his hair, with a sigh said. "Hello Manny. It's terrible, just terrible; everyone is in a state of shock."

Just then another car pulled up and parked. A slender man in sports coat and slacks got out carrying a black bag. Cleaning his glasses, he said. "Mornin' Manny."

Manny acknowledged motioning toward the room. "In there Fred."

"This Maria, was she employed here?" Manny asked.

Harry said, "Yes she is. Her name is Maria Alvarez and she works here as a maid and her room is on the other end of the building."

Manny heard the coroner's call and went into the room to converse with him. He returned to Harry and Charles and said. "It's official. Fred said it was a homicide."

This information was not a surprise to this group, but Charles thought it would be an added shock to the others. Manny motioned with his head toward the room next to Louisa's and directed a question to Harry. "Who occupies the other room?"

"That's Carlos Sanchez. He's a grounds keeper here."

Charles added, "He was Louisa's boyfriend."

"I'd like to talk to Maria and Carlos. Can you locate them Harry?"

"Maria is with Lisa and Doris, but I don't know where Carlos is. It appears he's missing."

Manny walked over to Carlos's room, examined the door, which was ajar, and walked in. When he came out he addressed the deputy sealing off the area around Louisa's room with yellow tape. "Deputy, include this room as the crime scene." Then he said to Charles and Harry, "I'm going to need a list of the names of the guests, employees and their addresses or where they can be located. Can you provide me with that Harry?"

"Actually, that would be my wife Lisa. She has all the records."

"Where's Maria? I want to talk to her first."

"They're in the lounge. I'll take you there." Harry led the group including a deputy to the lounge.

"I think I'm going to go home Lisa. I'm very frightened." Maria looked spent and spoke in a low voice.

"I'll call your family to come and get you."

“I am sorry to add to your problems but I’m too sad and frightened to work.”

“It’ll be all right. I’ll call in some temps.”

Doris spoke up and asked, “Could I help Lisa? I’ve had experience working at the reception desk in the hospital.”

“Thank you. That would be great. It would give me time to get replacements.”

They saw the group of men across the lounge led by Harry. Lisa stood up and approached them. Harry in a sober tone said. “Lisa, this is Lieutenant Manny Gomez and Sergeant Steve Rogers of the Sheriff’s Department.” Then, with a nod in the direction of the couch. “They want to talk to everyone.”

Manny stood and addressed the group who were now seated on the couch and chairs. “This is a homicide investigation and –”

Maria blurted out in disbelief. “Homicide! You mean murder? Oh my GOD!”

Doris reached out to console her.

“Yes, Maria, murder. That’s why we are going to need everyone’s cooperation. We’re going to be interviewing everyone. So Lisa if you would provide Sergeant Rogers with a list of guests and employees.” Manny pointed to the sergeant standing behind the chair. “He will coordinate the interviews.”

With a strained look, Lisa responded, “Yes, of course. Maria wants to go home. Will that be all right?”

“I think I’ll interview her first. While things are still fresh in her mind. Then so long as we have her address she can go. Harry, is there some place private where I can conduct the interviews?”

“Yes you can use my office, it’s just down the hallway.”

Manny placed his notebook and pen on Harry’s desk. “Steve, I’ll interview Maria, Harry, Lisa, and Charles and in that order. Have the deputies interview the guests and other employees. You follow up on the boyfriend Carlos."

"That does stand out. We don't have a smoking gun, but we might have a smoking Carlos." Steve said.

"Maybe with the information I get from the interviews and what you come up with we'll have a good picture of what happened."

"Did Fred say the cause of death?" Steve asked.

"From the bruises on her neck, he thinks strangulation. Ask Maria to come in."

Maria sat in the chair in front of the desk with her head resting on her hands.

"Are you, all right? Can I get you something?" Manny asked.

"I'll be all right."

"Maria, when did you last see Louisa?"

"It was after work when we were walking back to our rooms. Yesterday about five thirty."

"What did you talk about?"

"Just normal things. I asked her if she was going to the movies with Carlos."

"What was her answer?" Manny probed.

"No. She said she hadn't seen Carlos all day and asked if I had seen him. I told her I didn't see him since yesterday."

"Was she upset about that?"

"She seemed down. I thought maybe they had an argument."

"Did they argue a lot?" Manny asked.

"No, they seemed to get along."

"The rest of Saturday night did you hear or see anything?"

After hesitating, Maria said, "I was disturbed by a pack of howling coyotes. They sounded close so I went to the window and looked out."

Many leaned back in his chair. "Did you see them?"

"No."

"Did you see anything? Everything is important. Even little things."

Pausing to consider her reply, she said, "I saw someone going toward the back entrance to the Inn."

"Did you recognize the person?"

"No. It was just a dark figure. I thought it might be Harry but I don't know why."

"Tell me what happened on Sunday morning."

"I went to work and when I got there Louisa wasn't, so I went to her room to check. I thought she might have overslept. We were both scheduled to do the check out rooms that morning. She didn't answer the door so I thought she might be with Carlos. I went to Carlos's room but he wasn't there. I returned to Louisa's room and looked in the window. That's when I saw her sprawled on the bed and went for help." Her eyes filled with tears and in an almost whispered voice she asked. "Can I go home now?"

The other guests were either at the pool, hiking, or sightseeing. They were not in the lounge. The only people there were Harry, Charles, Doris, and Lisa. Maria went back to her room and waited for her family.

Doris broke from her conversation with Lisa and said to Charles. "I'm going to help Lisa at the front desk."

"Good. She's going to need help."

Lisa and Doris headed for the reception desk and Harry said. "That's kind of her. We're down three people."

"How will you manage?" Charles asked.

"We'll call MANPOWER for some temps. That will probably take a while so Lisa will call the other hotels and try to pick up off duty help."

"Mr. Wright." The voice came from a deputy emerging from the hallway.

"Yes."

"Lieutenant Gomez would like to talk to you."

"Fine. Excuse me, I'm on."

"How are things out there Harry?"

"It seems to be settling down. Lisa and Doris have turned their attention on running the Inn and Maria has gone back to her room to wait for her family."

"How about the guests?" Manny set down his coffee and picked up his pen.

"I don't know how much they know. They seem to be going about their business. I hope you will be as discreet as possible."

Nodding with a reassuring smile Manny replied. "We will. We've been in this type of situation many times." Leaning over the desk and positioning his notebook he got down to business. "Harry when was the last time you saw Louisa?"

"About eight thirty last night. I'm not sure of the exact time."

"Last night?" Manny looked up with interest. "Where?"

"In her room. I went there to confront her about some petty thefts we've been having."

"Why her?"

"I asked Charles to help me catch a thief. I marked some bills and he left them in his room. When he returned to his room some of the bills were missing. Later, I checked Lisa's work list and Maria signed off cleaning that room, but Lisa said she saw Louisa coming out of Charles's room."

"Wasn't that unusual to bring a guest into a situation like that? Why Charles?"

He's no ordinary guest. I mean he is, but his background isn't. He's a professor and has done consulting work for the Seattle Police Department."

"Very interesting. Did you find anything?"

"No. She emptied her purse and I scanned the bills with the penlight but I didn't find anything."

"When you arrived, could you tell if the door was locked?"

"Yes, it was. I could hear the action of the bolt."

Manny turned a page in his notebook and repositioned himself in his chair. "What was her attitude? Was she upset? Annoyed?"

"No. She cooperated."

"After that where did you go?"

"I went back to my office."

"Thank you, Harry. I'll look this over and if I have any questions I'll contact you. If you want to add anything call me." Manny stood up and handed Harry his card.

Lisa put down the phone and said to Doris. "I've got one borrowed for this afternoon and two temps staring tomorrow. If you need anything I'll be cleaning some rooms."

"I can do that too if you need me."

"Thanks. You're a big help and I appreciate it. Harry is not good at this type of work. He can train Carlos's replacement."

"Excuse me, Mrs. Wright." The deputy was standing at the counter addressing Doris. She motioned her head toward Lisa and said. "That would be Lisa."

"Oh, yes. Ma'am the lieutenant would like to talk to you. He knows you're very busy and said it won't take long."

She turned to Doris, took a tissue from the box on the desk and wiped her eyes. "It's so sad. She was such a sweet girl. It's a nightmare." She followed the deputy down the hallway.

Lisa looked strained as she sat down opposite Manny. Manny looked up from his notebook. "How you doing?"

"Can I get you something?" Lisa said, "Would you like a coffee? I'll call Anna."

"A coffee would be fine."

Lisa put down the phone, sat back in her chair and took a deep breath. "It's not just the scrambling around to fill a work schedule, I've done that, but not for such a horrible reason."

"Did you know about Harry's plan to catch a thief?"

"I did. He and Charles set a trap with marked bills."

Anna brought in the coffee and placed it on the desk. They both said, "Thank you."

"Harry said you directed him to Louisa."

"I did, but only after I brought him the check list and saw that Maria had signed off cleaning the room. I saw Louisa coming out of that room when I was leaving the supply room on that floor. At the time I had a passing feeling that it was odd and then when I was talking to Harry it came to me. She didn't have a cleaning cart and she wasn't carrying anything."

"Did Harry discuss his meeting with Louisa?"

"Yes, he told us about it this morning at breakfast on the patio. He said he didn't find anything."

"Did you know about Carlos's and Louisa's relationship?"

Lisa set down her coffee on the desk. "Yes, they were quite close. Everyone knew."

"Did you ever see them arguing?"

"No"

"When you did a background check on Carlos did you find any problems with the law?"

"No."

"Did he ever do this in the past? Just take off without any notice."

"No. He had good attendance."

"Thank you, Lisa, and also for the coffee."

Doris had just given directions and a map to a young couple at the desk when Charles walked up and said. "How you doing?"

"Fine, it's keeping my mind off things and I like the work. I like Lisa. She's easy to get along with."

"While you're doing that I'm going to offer my assistance to Manny. I don't know if he will accept it, but at least I'll be doing something."

Answering the phone Doris said in a professional voice. "Iron Door Inn, how may I help you? Oh, yes he is. I'll tell him." Setting down the phone she said. "Manny wants to see you."

Walking down the hallway, Charles was surprised at his feelings. In past cases it was an academic exercise that allowed him to remain detached. Now it was personal. Maybe it was because he was on the scene when it happened or seeing that young girl lifeless on the bed. Whatever it was, he was anxious about Manny's reaction to his offer of assistance.

"Charles, I understand from Harry that you have worked with the police. He said that's why he asked you to help him with his theft problem."

"That's true. It was Friday. The day after we arrived. We were talking on the patio and I told him I was a retired professor of psychology at the University of Washington."

"What did you do for the department?" Manny set his pen down and sat back in his chair.

"I gave seminars on Criminal Psychology and Motivation and consulted with them on homicides." Charles had an opening to make his offer. "I'd like to offer you my assistance on this case, if you're agreeable."

"I would welcome any assistance but considering the departments' budget restraints I don't think it would be approved." With a slight lowering of his head, he sighed, and his voiced showed disappointment.

Charles was quick to reply. "There would be no charge for my services. I feel compelled to help in any way I can."

"That's very generous of you Charles. I don't have any problem with it, but I'll have to run it by the captain and then do a background check."

"That's fine."

"Good, now let's discuss the case." Returning his attention to his notebook, he turned to a blank page. The interview was over and the theorizing began. "I think the first lead we have is Carlos's disappearance. It's too coincidental and statistics show that the perpetrator usually has a close connection to the victim. Do you agree?"

"Yes, and I think it'll be important to find out as much as we can about their relationship. Did you get any information from Maria?"

"She saw Louisa on Saturday night and said she seemed to be upset about not seeing Carlos. In general, she said they seem to get along." Manny's attention was drawn to the door.

Half opening the door, Sergeant Rodgers said. "Excuse me sir, I just want to let you know I'm back."

"Come in sergeant. Sergeant Rodgers this is Mr. Knowles. He has become an ally and will be assisting in the investigation."

Charles stood up and extended his hand. "Nice to meet you. You can call me Charles."

Manny motioned to a chair and said. "Pull up a chair and give us your report."

The sergeant was athletic looking with short hair and strong features. In a precise manner, he sat in his chair, notebook in hand, and began his report to his superior. "Carlos's room was empty of all personal items. There was nothing in the room to indicate where he might have gone. The lab team has finished their collecting and will give us the results later on both rooms. The coroner said the death occurred between 11:00 and 12:00 PM Saturday night. Cause of death was strangulation. The weapon was a small diameter cord with a spiral pattern.

Nothing of this type was found in either room but a search continues in the outside area."

His arms folded and one hand supporting his chin Manny asked. "Who was the last person to see Carlos?"

"That would be Frank Boone. He's the night security man. He saw him in an old Ford van leaving about 7:00 PM Friday night. On other occasions he had seen the same person pick up Carlos," the sergeant replied.

"Did he know his name?"

"Frank didn't but I checked with Maria before she left and she said that would be Reuben Ortega, Carlos's cousin."

"Louisa's door didn't appear to be broken into. Was it?" Charles said.

"No it wasn't. It was a dead bolt and no sign of forced entry."

Charles had another question, "What money did they find in Louisa's room?"

"The only money found in her room," the sergeant said, "was in her wallet. That contained about eighteen dollars."

"Charles, what are your thoughts so far? Anything strike you as odd or out of place, maybe untruths?" Manny asked.

Hesitating, Charles weighed his words carefully. "There are a few reactions that strike me as unusual and I'm going to give them some thought. They don't seem to have any connection right now, so I'm going to put them aside and look at the more obvious facts. Louisa is dead. Her boyfriend is missing. She seemed upset and didn't apparently know where he was. Her room wasn't broken into and nothing was missing that we know of. I think we're going to have to talk to Carlos."

"Carlos left Friday night and Louisa was killed on Saturday night. That would probably give him an alibi." Manny paused and then asked. "Do you think he came back?"

"It's possible. They could have had an argument, he left and returned later to make up and it turned violent, but it doesn't explain taking all his belongings and abandoning his job the night before. Carlos is the only one who can give us those answers."

"I agree. Sergeant put out an all-points bulletin for Carlos Sanchez wanted for questioning in the homicide of Louisa Perez and thought to be in the company of Reuben Ortega." Manny swiveled in his chair, closed his notebook and returned the pen he borrowed to the pencil holder. "I think that's it for today, Charles. In the morning after I review all the information the other deputies have collected I'll give you a call. Let's hope the solution is as simple as it appears."

Charles smiled. "I'm afraid that we both realize that that would not be a common reality."

"Oh, there you are. I was hoping you would be coming out soon. I'm hungry." Doris had been relieved from her front desk activities by the night clerk. "I wasn't sure when you would be out so I asked Lisa if we could have sandwiches sent up to the room."

The night air was dry and warm. The mountains silhouetted in front of the darkening sky. The swooping flight of the nighthawks could be seen around the lights illuminating the pool area Doris and Charles had finished their sandwiches and now sipped their coffee. Charles leaned back in his chair and held his coffee mug with both hands, he said. "Manny accepted my offer to assist him."

"That's great. It will be good for you and it will be satisfying to know you did something. I know helping Lisa has diverted my attention from the horror of it all. Does Manny have a theory?"

"The focus is on the missing boyfriend. He packed up and left Friday night. Maria gave information that Louisa didn't know about it and she was in fact disturbed by it. If you add the statistical fact that murders are usually committed by someone the victim knew, you would have to deduce that Carlos is the best lead."

"What's his plan?"

"He also knows that Carlos is in the company of a man named Reuben Ortega, so he has issued an all-points bulletin for both of them."

"It all seems so cut and dry. What are your thoughts?" Doris said.

"I agree with Manny and the action he has taken, but I don't feel comfortable with it. It's not something I can talk to him about because it's not concrete."

"For instance?"

"The motive. I can't establish a reasonable motive. Oh, sure lovers do commit violent crimes, but he had left the scene. There has been no information about previous violence. There's something missing. Maybe I'm not used to straight forward cases."

"This might be a new experience for you."

"Finding Carlos would be big help." Doris and Charles both stood up and walked over to the rail to view the rising moon from behind the mountain.

Charles returned to his room from an early breakfast with Doris, who went directly to work at the front desk. He answered his cell phone.

"They found Carlos," Manny said.

"Good news. Where did they find him?"

"In the state prison hospital."

Charles was taken back. "In jail?"

"Yes. I'm going up to Florence to interview him. Would you like to join me?"

"Would I? That would be great. How did he end up in the jail hospital?"

"I'll tell you all about it on the way to Florence. Can you be ready in about a half hour?"

"Sure. I'll be waiting in the lounge."

On the way to the front desk to tell Doris his head was filled with questions. What was he doing in jail? Did he confess? Why was he in the hospital? Did he have a confrontation with the police? Lisa was at the desk with Doris. "Good morning Lisa. I have some good news. They found Carlos."

Both Doris and Lisa looked amazed. Lisa said, "Great. That was fast. Where did they find him? Did he tell them anything?"

"He's in the state prison hospital. "

Doris repeated. "State prison hospital?"

"I'm going up there with Manny to interview him."

"That was nice of him to invite you." Pursing her lips, Doris added. "I see you two did some professional bonding yesterday."

"We did. I think we can work well together. Lisa, where's Harry? I'd like to give him the news."

"He's going over the work routine with the new maintenance man. I'll tell him when he comes back."

Manny sat in the back seat with Charles and Sgt. Rodgers drove the police cruiser on route #79 toward Florence. It was a pleasant 60-mile drive void of traffic and through the Falcon valley. The low desert vegetation gave way for spacious views in all directions and the mountains provided the background.

"This is what we know so far." Manny began his summary. "Reuben, Carlos's cousin, picked him up on Friday night for a planned trip to California. Saturday morning, Reuben also picked up six illegal immigrants. He picked them up at a collection point in the desert off of Interstate 10. It's about a 3 mile ride over a dirt road."

"I've heard about organized gangs called coyotes, was he one of these?" Illegal immigrant smuggling was a crime Charles had only read about.

"No, he wasn't and hence the problem. These coyote gangs are well organized and are as vicious as the drug gangs."

"How was he able to pick these people up?"

"Some gang members guide them across the desert on foot to the collection area. This is phase one and they are paid separately. In phase two other gang members pick them up and take them to Los Angeles or Phoenix.

"Wouldn't the gang members know each other?"

"Good question. This is a weak link in their system and it leaves them open for hijacking. The foot coyotes leave them there and start back to the border. They don't know when the road coyotes are going to pick them up. It depends on border patrol activity and roadblocks. They pick them up when the time is right."

"Or in this case anybody whoever wanted to cut into the business." Charles said.

"Normally it could be done without high risk but in this case the foot coyotes were not far from the collection point and heard the Ford van. They rushed back only in time to see the vehicle and part of the license plate. They called gang members in Phoenix, who immediately set out to intercept them on Interstate 10. Driving south, in a Ford Explorer, they spotted the Ford van going north on the other lane. They crossed the median pull along side and open fired with automatic weapons."

"My GOD, that's unbelievable" Charles said, "The people on the highway must have been shocked'?"

"Fortunately, none of them were hurt." Manny continued in his concise manner. "At the same time the gang opened fire, the car in front of Reuben pulled out in the passing lane causing the Ford Explorer to decelerate. When Reuben was hit, the Ford van swerved to the left into the Explorer, careened and tumbled them both into the median. Reuben and three of the immigrants were killed. Carlos and the other three immigrants in the Ford van and two of the gang members were seriously hurt.

They're searching the desert for the third gang member who got away."

Charles had never heard of an incident like this. It happened in broad daylight on a major highway and with such reckless violence. The only association he had was the movies depicting the violence in the days of prohibition. "How seriously was Carlos hurt?

"They have taken him out of the intensive care unit to a room, but he is still in critical condition. He received a bullet wound to his shoulder and neck. His right arm also was shot and the accident caused injuries to his head and leg. He's conscious, but I don't think we are going to be given much time for questioning. With that in mind I think we should decide upon the most important questions." What questions would you like answered?"

"Now that we know he couldn't have murdered Louisa, it's a fresh investigation. His disappearance sent us off in the wrong direction. I wonder if the murderer was counting on that. Our questions will have to be relative to his relationship with Louisa; her activities and mental state leading up to the murder."

Charles had an eerie feeling when he saw the large fenced in building standing all alone in the open desert. The three of them were quiet as the cruiser pulled into the State Prison and a touch of claustrophobia gripped him as they were checked through the gate. On the way to the hospital as each door or gate slammed behind him the claustrophobic grip tightened a notch. This sterile atmosphere brought him thoughts of how the simplest things warm our every day lives and physical containment is a far more severe punishment than most imagine. At the nurse's station the doctor briefed them on Carlos's condition and gave them a time limit for the interview and then an orderly showed them to the room.

Carlos's shoulder, neck and left arm were bandaged and his face was bruised. There was fear in his eyes as Manny made the introductions and before Manny finished he blurted out. "I didn't know about the smuggling until we were on the road. I couldn't do anything about it then. Maybe I should have a lawyer here?"

"We're not here for that Carlos. Do you know about Louisa's death?"

"Yes my aunt told me. I didn't have anything to do with that either. I was here in the hospital."

At this point the orderly came back with a chair for Sergeant Rodgers who positioned himself discreetly by the window for his note taking. Charles and Manny pulled their chairs to the side of the bed and closer to Carlos. Charles, in an attempt to mollify Carlos and take his focus off Manny, said, "What was your relationship with Louisa?"

"We were going together. You know that or you wouldn't be here."

"Yes, but how long did you know each other? Was it a good relationship?"

Charles expected a natural resistance of authority from Carlos and was relieved when after a pause he said, "About six months, we met at the Inn." For the first time his eyes softened. We got along for awhile, but then she started getting on my nerves."

"How so?" Manny said as he and Charles reacted with heightened interest.

"I told her about Reuben planning to move to California and I thought it was a great idea. Maybe we could go with him and get better jobs. She was excited about it and agreed to go. She asked when we would go and I told her it'd be in a couple of months. It would take that long for me to save up enough money to get started in California. I told her that with both of us saving our money we would have plenty for expenses. She said she didn't know how she would do that on her small check and she was already sending some money home. I said it was easy. You have it under your nose every day. That's when I gave her a plan to steal from the rooms. She wasn't cool about the idea, but I told her if she wanted to go that's what she had to do."

"Did she agree?' Charles asked.

"She did." Carlos's demeanor had changed during the interview. Charles, being a romantic, thought it was brought on by his feelings about Louisa.

Manny adjusting his chair and crossing his leg said. "When did she start getting on your nerves?"

"In the last few weeks it started to bother her. She had never done anything like that. Last Thursday night she went postal. I thought she might tell someone. After that, I decided not to take her. I didn't need all that emotional shit."

Charles noticed a wince of pain in Carlos's eyes. He knew they didn't have much time. He pressed on. "When did you leave with Reuben?"

"He called me Friday night and said it was on for early Saturday morning. I didn't know why so quick, but I asked if he could pick me up then so I wouldn't have to face Louisa. I stayed at his house Friday night."

"Where did she keep this money?" Charles asked.

"You know this is tiring. How long are you going to ask me questions?" Carlos was showing signs of strain.

Manny answered, "Not much longer. You know we're trying to find out who murdered Louisa. You can help us Carlos. Then he repeated Charles's question. "Where did she keep the money?"

"In one of those bank deposit bags. I gave it to her. She kept it in the top dresser drawer. About once a week she gave it to me. She didn't like keeping it in her room."

Charles remembered that no money was found in the room and that Harry checked the money in her bag. "When was the last time she gave you the money?"

In a weakening voice Carlos said, "The Sunday before I left."

Realizing their time was running out, Charles asked two questions. "Did anybody else know she had the money in her room? Were there any jealous ex boyfriends?"

"Not that I know of." Was Carlos's answer to both questions when the orderly came in the room and without preamble said, "Times up."

Manny looked out of the cafe window at the old historic downtown of Florence and said. "We're lucky we didn't lose him in that shoot out. If we did we would be high and dry."

Sergeant Rodgers said, with a pause between bites of his hamburger, "I didn't expect him to be so cooperative. At first, he seemed uptight, a little hostile."

"I think when he realized we weren't there to question him about his present problems he settled down."

Charles turned to Manny and said. "I think the information about Louisa stealing and keeping the money in her room is important, plus the fact it wasn't found in the room."

"That's true and it gives us a starting point for a new theory, but there was probably only a few hundred dollars in the bag." Manny looked bewildered and contemplated his own question,

"People have killed for less," the sergeant said, "and the killer probably didn't' know how much there was in the bag."

"It does raise a lot of questions," Charles said, "but as Manny said, without it we would be high and dry. Now we've got a lot to think about. Did the killer go there just to steal the money? He had to know she was in there. Was the intent murder for some unknown reason and the theft of the bag a cover?"

Manny reached for his wallet and the check at the same time and said. "Nothing personal Charles, I know you're on vacation, but I hope this keeps you awake tonight." He stood up with a broad smile.

"If I do, I'll give you a call." Charles replied chuckling.

"Thanks, although I'd have to put you on call waiting."

Outside walking to the cruiser on the boarded walkway Manny said. "This town looks like the old western town you see in the movies. It makes you feel like you should be wearing a cowboy hat and boots."

"Manny– you do wear a cowboy hat and boots." Charles released the somberness of the day with a burst of laughter.

"Oh, that's right." Manny reacted with a self-conscious smile and an involuntary chuckle. "That's right, I have to live up to that image of a sheriff for you northern folk."

The trip back seemed to pass quickly for Charles. He though it might be attributed to the fact that the case had taken a whole new turn. It was no longer a case of a lovers quarrel gone badly, but a case that presented a substantial challenge. Manny, in his kidding was right on, thoughts of the case would be bouncing around in his mind all night.

As the cruiser pulled into the parking area of the Inn, Manny said. "Sergeant, I have an appointment. Drop me off at my car and then I want you to make a copy of your notes and bring them back to Charles. He might want to look at them tonight. I'd like to review everything with you Charles, in the morning, if that's agreeable with you?"

"Sounds good to me. Walking up the steps to the entrance of the Inn, he realized it was a long time since he had been involved in solving a case. It energized him and more so than in the past.

Lisa said, "You've been a great help Doris and I really appreciate it. Things are running smooth again, so if you want to get back to vacationing you can."

"That will depend on what they found out from Carlos."

"How so?"

"It's possible he didn't commit the murder. If that's the case, Charles attention will be on solving the case, not vacationing."

In a sympathetic tone Lisa said. "That's too bad."

"Not really. I find it fascinating. It probably wouldn't be if he didn't take me into his confidence, but he does. If that happens I'd need a favor from you."

"From me?" Lisa said with a chuckle and an incredulous look. "Like what?"

"Well I like to keep busy and it would be fun to work on those new flower boxes on the patio."

"No problem. I'd be glad to have you do it. I know the flowers are not up to par, I don't have time to do it, and that's not our yard workers forte."

Doris heard footsteps and turned to see Charles. "Oh, you're back. How did it go?"

Wanting to be more discreet when he answered her, Charles went through the half door and further into the office. "Carlos is not the murderer. A lot has happened since Friday night. Immigrant smugglers attacked them, killing Reuben, and leaving Carlos wounded and in the hospital. We are going to have to look elsewhere for our murderer."

Both women were amazed. A sense of fear showed in Lisa's eyes. "That means the murderer could be someone here. Somebody we know."

"Or it could be someone from outside. Maybe from her past. We don't know. All the possibilities will have to be considered." Charles hoped that the 'someone' from outside possibility would give Lisa a bit of relief. "Is Harry around? I'd like to bring him up to date."

"I don't know where he is. Maybe it would be a good idea to have dinner together and you could do that then. It's homemade pizza night on the patio or we could eat in the dining room, if you prefer."

Getting an approval look from Doris, Charles said, "Pizza on the patio sounds great. What time?"

"About six thirty."

"Let's watch the news. They might have more on the Interstate 10 shootout." Charles turned on the TV and having said that had visions of the old west.

Doris came out of the bathroom and said. "Why do I have the feeling you have a lot more to tell me?"

"Because you know I'm discreet, especially concerning a case." Charles found the local station and sat in the chair next to the patio door.

Doris got comfortable on the bed with two pillows under her head. "Oh, it feels so good to get off my feet. Would you open those drapes, it's a little dark in here."

Charles opened the drapes and described the events that led to Carlos being in the prison hospital. The newscaster who announced an update on the Interstate 10 drive by shooting interrupted him. "The Pinal County Sheriff's Department has just announced the arrest of the third gang member suspected in the Saturday drive by shooting on Interstate 10. He was found in the desert and in very bad condition. Suffering from dehydration, exposure and other injuries he received in the accident, he was taken to the Florence State Prison hospital where he will be held for questioning. His identity is not known at this time. Four people were killed and six others were injured in the shoot out. When we come back, John will gave us the five day forecast–"

"I can't image driving down the highway and having that happen. To think we came down the same road on Thursday. Was Carlos a gang member?" Doris said.

"They're not sure of his implication, of course he's denying any involvement." Charles turned the volume down with the remote. "He did give us-"

With a solemn look Doris interrupted, "Did he know about Louisa?"

"Yes, he did, and I think we got some useful information out of him. He said Louisa was stealing from the rooms."

"Louisa! Harry said he didn't find any marked money in her room. How did he know she was stealing?"

"Because he was the one who talked her into it and she was giving him the money to keep for their trip to California–which she didn't take."

"Did she change her mind?"

"No, he got annoyed with her and decided not to take her." There was a knock on the door and Charles got up to answer it.

Opening the door he faced a young man who said. "Good evening Mr. Knowles, a Sergeant Rodgers left this at the front desk for you."

"What's that?" Doris said.

Closing the door and returning to his chair, Charles answered. "Manny had the sergeant make copies of all the interview notes. He suspected I might be giving it a lot of thought tonight. They're very efficient; I enjoy working with them."

"It looks like the feeling is mutual."

"I hope so." He paused to flip through the pages and stopped at the notes on Maria's interview and then turned to Harry's. "I have already found something interesting. When Maria last saw Louisa she seemed upset, but when Harry went to her room she was calm."

"Interesting, but I have to get ready for dinner."

The patio was decorated with an Italian theme in keeping with the Inn's practice of having two nights a week designated as theme nights on the patio. The atmosphere was colorful and festive. Buffet tables holding a variety of pizzas, under warming lights, were set up on one side of the large glass doors, while on the other side the tables held desserts. Leaning against the stonewall, separating the patio and the pool, an accordion player brought life to the theme.

"Everything seems back to normal." Lisa said. She and Harry had arrived first.

Harry looked at the new waitress in a costume appropriate to the evening and said, "Is that one of the replacements?"

"Her name is Cheryl and she's a university student. How are we doing? You haven't mentioned anything about our financial problem since last week."

With a smug look and confident tone Harry said, "Oh, Its not as bad as I thought, by controlling the expenses and the inventory, I think we'll be all right. The occupancy ratio is high and advanced bookings are up."

"Isn't that something about Carlos being involved in that shoot out and being in the hospital at the time of the murder?" Not waiting for a reply, Lisa called the waitress and continued. "We might as well have our drinks, while we are waiting."

"I caught some of that on the news," Harry said, "but had no idea Carlos was involved. It's incredible, who else would do it? It had to be someone she knew from off the property, probably a jealous boyfriend. It wouldn't surprise me if it was drug related. Well, perhaps our unassuming bird watcher, turned crime guru, will run the culprit to ground."

"You may mock him, but Lieutenant Gomez has a lot of respect for him. He consults with him and brought him to the interview with Carlos. I think it's nice he wants to meet with us and bring us up to date. Oh, here they come."

The couples exchanged greetings and Doris said that she loved the music, lighting, colorful streamers and other decorations. "I love your theme nights. The last time we were here the themes were German and Mexican."

"Thank you. I think the favorite for the guests is Mexican night with the mariachi music." Lisa stood up and suggested that they go up to the buffet table and they all followed her lead.

A light conversation was carried on during the meal, but when Charles came back from his second trip to the buffet table, Harry said. "I understand you had a very interesting day in Florence?"

Choosing his words carefully, Charles gave an account of the events leading up to Carlos's internment in the prison hospital, leaving out details pertinent to the case, such as Louisa was a thief and there is a missing money bag.

"Extraordinary, but as I was telling Lisa, it probably was someone she knew before she came here." With a furrowed brow and questioning eyes, Harry continued, "What do you think?"

"It's very possible, but we have little to go on. You were the last one to see her that we can question. In your interview you mentioned the door was locked." Charles was treading lightly, he didn't want to be intimidating or appear arrogant. "The police report showed that her key was in the room. I noticed, Lisa, that you have a metal key box on the wall in your office. Is that for master keys?"

"Yes, it holds keys for inside the building, including the guest rooms."

"Who has the key for that?"

"One key is in the office for use by the day and night clerks and the housekeeper." Lisa answered.

The waitress appeared at Lisa's side and asked. "Can I bring you anything else to drink, ma'am."

Lisa responded, "Does everyone want coffee?" With comments of approval from everyone and a request for decaf from Charles, the waitress glided away.

Harry picked up where Lisa left off. "There's another box in my office holding miscellaneous keys and the duplicate keys for the staff rooms. That's also where I keep the key for that box. Louisa could have made a key for someone. Did she give one to Carlos?"

"No, he didn't have one. Harry is that box used much?" Charles thought it could be the answer to how the murderer got in?

"No it isn't."

"After we have finished up here, do you think we could check and see if the key to the box is still in your desk?"

"I'd be glad to."

The last few minutes at the table were spent listening to the accordion player sing O Sole Mio. When he had finished Doris said, "That was great! It was a delightful evening. Thank you."

Harry went right to his desk and switched on the desk lamp. To Charles's surprise, instead of going into his desk drawer, he picked up a cylindrical, metal, pen and pencil holder. Holding the pens and pencils in one hand, he dumped the remaining contents onto the desktop. A couple of rubber bands, some paper clips, a key and a decorative silver object, all fell out.

Charles noticed the latter and said, "That's a beautiful piece of work. Is it a bola tie clasp?"

"It is. It was done by one of our local silversmiths, and this is the key to the box."

"I'm surprised that you don't keep the key locked in your desk." That seemed the logical place, to Charles.

"I could keep it in the safe too, but I think that would be overkill. It's not used much and if I send someone in for it they don't have to go through my desk looking for it."

"Then someone else might have known of its location. Well, let's check the box and see if any keys are missing."

"It's possible." Harry opened the black metal key box attached to the wall and examined the contents.

"They're all here." Pointing to one of the hooks he added. "That's the one to Louisa's room."

"At least now we know that someone else could have gained access."

Harry locked the box, replaced the key in the pencil holder, and moved toward the door. "I still think it was someone from outside."

"But there was no sign of forced entry."

Now standing in the hallway Harry said, "They could have picked the lock."

"They could have." Charles realized Harry was not thinking through his theory, so he refrained from saying that, if he did it would be unlikely he would reverse the process when he left.

Doris returned to the room and was sitting on the patio when Charles came back and joined her. "Was the duplicate key still there?"

"Yes it was, but the key to the metal box was on Harry's desk."

"On his desk?"

"Yes, in a metal pen and pencil holder."

"Well, at least it was hidden," said Doris

"Others could have known about it. On occasion he said he sent an employee after a maintenance key."

"You seem to be following the key instead of the money, as they say."

"There aren't any leads to the money," after a pause Charles went on, "but a key had to be used to get the money. Louisa's key was found in the room and the door was locked when we got there."

"Didn't Harry open the door?'

"Yes, he did and I just thought he had a master key, but now knowing there's not a master key but a duplicate, it puts a different light on it." Charles stood up and moved to the railing. He turned to Doris and gave a ponderous sigh.

Doris stopped her knitting and said. "Why? I should think the owner having a key would be normal."

"If it was one to the maintenance rooms or the supply room yes, but a duplicate key to Louisa's room on Sunday morning."

"That is suspicious, but there must be some explanation."

"There's something else too. It could have a simple explanation but it's been bothering me since I left Harry's office."

"What's that?"

"When Harry retrieved the box key from the pen and pencil holder a clasp fell out onto the desk, a decorative silver one that is used on a bola tie. I wondered if he wore a bola tie and if he did where the cord that the clasp attaches to was."

Doris perked up and said. "He did. I saw a picture of Lisa and Harry on Lisa's desk and he was wearing one."

"Can you describe it?"

"Yes, it was good size, silver, and had red and green inlay."

"I wonder when it was taken." Charles said, not expecting an answer.

"I can tell you that too. When I was admiring it, Lisa said it was taken at a fundraiser two weeks ago. The other man in the picture is a local TV celebrity."

"Two weeks ago. What happened to the cord?"

Looking perplexed Doris said, "That I can't help you with. What does it look like?"

"Oh, it's a strip of leather, or it could be made of other material, that's the tie part of it. It's similar to a necklace. The bola, or clasp, holds it together. Sometimes the ends of the cord are banded in metal."

"I told Lisa it was so southwestern to see a man wearing a bola tie, and she told me Harry likes them and hasn't worn a regular tie since he's been out here. Is this something that could be relevant to the case?"

"I'm going to discuss it with Manny tomorrow. You know they haven't found the murder weapon."

"Murder weapon!"

"Louisa was strangled."

"Oh, that's too bizarre to think about. I mean what reason? I'm going to turn in now. How about you?"

"I am going to read the notes before I meet with Manny in the morning. Good night." Charles suppressed a strong urge to call Manny right then.

Charles did have a good night sleep after reviewing the notes, contrary to his previous habits in such circumstances. After he had a pleasant breakfast on the patio with Doris, Sergeant Rodgers arrived to take him to Manny's office. When they arrived the sergeant brought him to the office. Manny greeted him warmly. "Morning Charles," pausing with a playful grin, "Did you sleep well?"

"Yes, I did, as a matter of fact. Surprisingly since my mind seems to be bombarded with snippets of tantalizing information."

"Whoa, whoa, snippets, you are in a state Charles." Laughing, Manny gathered up some books and papers on his desk. "I think we will use the meeting room where we can spread out and won't be interrupted."

Charles placed the notes on the tabletop and shuffled them into order. Then he took out his own notebook, flipped it open and asked. "As the case stands now, what issues do you see as needing to be resolved?"

"All right," Manny picked up his pencil and doodled on a pad, considering his reply, he said. "First, Carlos said there was a money bag, but there was no money bag containing stolen money found in the room. Second, Harry said he didn't find any stolen money in the room."

Charles nodded his approval and said. "Two good issues. I'd like to add two more. The fact that Harry had a key to Louisa's room on Sunday morning is unusual. Also, I would like to add an underlying psychological issue that is conflicting in the testimony. Carlos and Maria both claim she was in an upset condition, Harry said she was calm. Knowing from Carlos that she was stealing, and the fact that he left her, it just does not make sense that she was calm."

Manny looked incredulous and said, "Harry? What possible motive? There couldn't have been much money. Those thoughts aside, I think the answer will be in finding the missing bag."

"Now for some new information that I discovered yesterday. Since following the money doesn't seem probable, at this point, I think we have to follow the key, which was used to get to the money. We know Harry opened that door. Inquiring about the key I found out he used a duplicate key, which happened to be in his pocket Sunday morning, that's kept in a locked Sentry box mounted on the wall of his office." Charles, with a steady gaze, waited for a response.

"Not a master key, interesting, and a good question to put to Harry." Manny made a note on his pad.

"Now, when I was in his office he retrieved the key for the Sentry box out of the pen and pencil holder on his desk. When we checked the box the key to her room was there."

Following the trend of thought Manny said, "But because of where the Sentry box key was kept it opens up the possibility someone else could have used it."

"Absolutely. But another interesting thing happened when he retrieved it from the pencil holder. Holding the pens and pencils in one hand he dumped the contents on the desk. The key fell out along with some small items and a good size bola clasp."

"A clasp? No tie?" Manny asked,

"No tie. Just a clasp of a bola tie which I was informed by my observing wife he wore to a charity affair two weeks ago."

"It appears we have raised a cloud of suspicion." Manny stood up, moved to the window, and adjusted the window blind. "It's almost time for lunch. Do you want to go out, or have sandwiches brought in?"

"Eat in. Clouds are funny things, one minute they're there, and the next minute they're gone."

"I agree." Manny said and picked up the phone. "Drink?"

"Diet Coke."

After he replaced the phone, Manny stretched, leaned back, and ran his hands through his hair. Charles stroked his beard. It seemed ritualistic. Manny broke the silence. "The motive, which we don't have, would have to be very strong to take such a risk. Carlos's room was next to hers and Harry knew they had a relationship."

"On the porch that morning," Charles said, "when you asked if you could talk to Maria and Carlos, Harry said that Carlos was missing. It's a natural conclusion that he was aware of this when Carlos didn't show up for work Saturday morning, but it is also possible that he learned of this from Louisa on his visit about eight thirty Saturday night. A second visit, for reasons we don't know, might not have been so risky."

"You seem to be building up to something," Manny said, "What is it?"

Charles said in a solemn voice, "We need a search warrant for Harry's office."

"Search warrant!" Manny cleared his throat and went on. "On what basis?"

"The murder weapon for one, and there's a safe in that office that could be holding evidence, a bank bag and marked money. I believe that after Harry returned that night from his first visit with Louisa, something happened to initiate the act of murder. The bola tie was a perfect weapon for strangulation. It is also very easy to conceal. Before I continue, there's one thing I would like to check. I want to ask Maria one question."

"That's easy. We have her number." Manny picked up the phone. "Yes, Maria Alvarez. When you contact her, put her right through to me. Thank you."

"Hello Maria, this is Lieutenant Gomez, how are you? Good, Maria, Charles Knowles is working with us on the case and he would like to ask you a question." Manny handed the phone to Charles. "Hello Maria, how you doing? Good, yes we heard Carlos is recovering. No he didn't. Maria my question is what made you identify Harry as the person you saw outside your window that night? It was dark, you couldn't see any facial features, but Harry came to mind. Could it have been his clothing? Can you describe what he was wearing?"

Maria hesitated and then said, "It was his jacket. It was a nice jacket. I liked the style. The color was green. I've seen him wear it before. Yea, I think that's it. The general appearance, the way he was walking, and the jacket."

"Well, you were right. We know it was Harry, but we just wanted to see if you could tell us what he was wearing, and you did. Thank you, Maria."

Charles handed the phone back to Manny and said. "In the corner of Harry's office is a coat rack with a green jacket hanging on it. I believe the cord part of the bola tie is in that jacket. It's clever in its simplicity. He was going to attach it back on the clasp, but for whatever reason, he never did. If he had, it would have been perfect, it would be hidden in plain sight."

"Do we have enough for a search warrant?" Charles asked.

"You have presented a very logical set of possibilities, but it just seems to float in the air without a motive to anchor it. I don't think that should stop us though."

Charles was relieved to see that Manny was interested. "Then how do we go about convincing a judge?"

"I think we can give him all this new information and the fact that the original search did not include Harry's office. I'm going to run it by the captain first and get his opinion."

"Do you think it can be done without Harry's knowledge? I'd like to keep him in the dark as to our suspicions. If we don't find anything it would put him on guard."

Manny stood, gathered his notes and said. "That's a chance we'll have to take. Even if we did it when he was off the premises, whoever was in charge of the property at that time, or someone seeing us would probably tell him."

"How soon do you think it can be done? My concern now is that he might move something out of there."

"A sense of urgency will be part of the request. The longer we delay the search, the bigger the possibility of loss of evidence. Once we have the authority we will move right away. I'll call you as soon as I get it."

Doris and Lisa were busy planting and rearranging flowers in the flowers boxes on the stonewalls on each side of the three steps leading down to the pool area. The colors of the sun-drenched flowers were intensified by the contrasting shadow of a cotton wood tree across the patio floor. Doris, wearing her wide brim hat and gardening gloves, said, "I think this one just needs a couple more plants and a little fertilizer."

Setting down a flat of flowers Lisa said. "I am enjoying this. I wouldn't have been able to commit so much time to it, but with you working on it I am able to come out and help whenever I can."

"Saw Charles going off with the police, hope he wasn't arrested." Harry said with a smug smile.

Both ladies heard him before they saw him. Doris answered, "Oh, he went off to meet Manny."

"And he's not back yet, they must have had a lot to talk about."

Doris continued her work and said. "I suppose so."

Harry pressed on. "I wonder if they came up with anything new."

"How quizzical you are today." Lisa said and then added with a look of reprehension, "You haven't even mentioned our project. What do you think?"

"It's beautiful. You two make a good team."

"Oh, look who's here. Maybe Charles can satisfy your curiosity."

Unlike Harry, Charles was impressed with the work. "That really looks great. So colorful."

Harry said, "It seems you had a long session Charles, were there any new developments?"

"Not really. We just went over the facts in detail. It's time consuming but it's necessary for formulating any theory."

"And did you come up with any?"

"Not yet." Charles said, but was thinking we did and a strong one at that. "Well, I think the murderer is miles away by now. I, for one, would like a little diversion from all this. Lisa would you like to go to the movies tonight?"

Lisa perked up. "Great idea. You two want to join us?"

Charles answered, "I've some things to do." Then to Doris, "But if you want to."

"No, no thanks. I'm trying to finish a sweater I'm knitting. If we relocate out here, I think I'll switch to needlepoint."

Charles was thankful that Doris recognized his intent, that he didn't want to go to the movies, but she couldn't possibly know it was because they may be needed for other activities that night. Back in the room, after leaving Lisa and Doris to finish up, he was trying to calm himself. There was reason for excitement. What an opportunity for the search, although he had to be realistic, what were the chances that the warrant would be approved in time to take advantage of their absence? With a heavy sigh, he picked up the phone and dialed.

"Manny here, oh hello Charles, what's up?"

"They're going to the movies tonight. I know it might be too soon for a search, but I had to let you know just in case."

"I'm glad you did. I'm on my way back to the station with the warrant. What time are they going?"

"I don't know. I'll have to find out and let you know." With a sinking feeling, Charles felt he dropped the ball. It was a key piece of information he could have picked up quite innocently when the subject was raised on the patio.

His thought was interrupted by Doris's voice as she entered the room. "I couldn't wait to get up here so you could fill me in. You not wanting to go to the movies, I knew something was up."

Doris listened in amazement as Charles described the meeting and his theory. "Manny was very receptive when he heard the new information and thought taken as a whole it was a strong theory. Strong enough for him to request and get a search warrant."

A perplexed Doris said, "I have a hard time even imagining someone doing such a thing, let alone it being Harry. I know you're experienced, but how you can possibly work up a theory from nothing, I'll never know."

"It's just a theory, we haven't found anything yet. In a case like this, without an obvious motive, you have to follow the statistical probabilities. That was Carlos, but he couldn't have done it, although we did learn from him that money was involved. We can't follow the money so we have to follow the one thing that would have to be used to get it. The key to Louisa's room, which leads us to Harry's office. In a sense we found the key, can the money or murder weapon be far behind. Now we have a search warrant."

"That was fast," Doris said.

"Manny is very efficient."

"When will they do it?"

"I just got off the phone with him and told him they are going to the movies. I couldn't give him the time." Charles gave a heavy sigh and added. "I missed that one."

Doris perked up and said, "That's no problem. Seven to ten."

"Incredible! You always come up with pertinent information. How did you learn that?"

"After we put away our gardening tools and supplies, we stopped by the office. That's when I heard Lisa tell the night clerk she would be off the property from seven to ten. They were going to the movies. Now I think I'll change and get ready for dinner."

A very pleased Charles had already picked up the phone. "I'll give Manny that information."

They dined on the patio and Charles sat facing the glass patio doors. He wanted to watch the activity in the lobby. Maybe he would see them leave. Manny said he would call him when he arrived. Every nerve in his body was tense and he knew this was a pivotal stage in the case.

"Charles you're so tense," Doris said, "Relax. It's so pleasant out here. You can't hurry it along. It'll happen."

"You're right, but when your theory is about to be tested, you become quite anxious." He took Doris's advice and made a few, slow, deep breathes and then he became aware of the beautiful night. He turned to look at all the other guests enjoying the fresh air and the sound of the new cottonwood leaves fluttering in the light breeze.

Everything was ready, the paper work, the search team, Manny and Sergeant Rodgers. They sat in the cruiser waiting for word from a spotter who was in a position to observe anyone coming from the Inn. Then they heard his voice. "They just passed."

"Good," Manny said, "follow at a safe distance. Let us know if anything changes." He then spoke to the search team, "We'll wait about ten minutes, in case they forgot something."

"Like last year," Sergeant Rodgers said, "that was embarrassing."

In Rm. #16, Charles was pacing. In an effort to distract him, Doris set down her knitting, got up and turned on the TV. She picked up the remote, handed it to him and said. "Why don't you find something to watch? It might settle you down." When Charles heard the knock on the door, he knew he wouldn't be settling down.

When Manny and Charles reached Harry's office, the search team was already at work and Sergeant Rodgers was standing outside the office door. They paused inside the office, Manny put on a pair of latex gloves and handed Charles a pair. Manny sat in the desk chair and the team worked on the safe. Charles walked directly to the coat rack in the corner and with a sigh of satisfaction withdrew a cord with ends tipped with silver ferrules. He returned to the desk and dropped the cord on it. Manny turned and said. "What have we here?"

"One half of a bola tie." Charles reached down, picked up the pen and pencil holder, and dumped the contents on the desk.

Manny picked up the silver clasp. "The second half of a bola tie. You called that one. Lee, bag these two items and make a note the cord could be the murder weapon."

"Safe is opened Lieutenant."

"Good job, John."

"Do you want everything taken out?" John said.

Manny leaning over in his chair said. "Not yet. Just hand me that bank bag." He turned to Charles who was sitting in front of the desk and said. "I suppose it's not uncommon for a businessman to have a bank bag in his safe."

"I guess what's inside will tell the story." Charles replied.

Manny opened the bag, pulled out the contents, and spread the bills and a white ticket on the desk. "What's this? A lottery ticket."

"That's my ticket! That was with the money Louisa stole. It was missing. I couldn't find it anywhere."

"We'll have to check this money with the infra-red light."

"You don't have to." Charles reached in his pocket and pulled out the list of the serial numbers he had made of the marked bills.

Manny was impressed. He took the list and checked the bills. "They check out. These are the bills stolen by Louisa."

"What do we do now?" Charles asked staring at the bills.

"We send back the search team and wait to make an arrest."

Charles, trying to visualize the actual arrest said, "When will you take him?"

Manny said, "I don't want the vehicle stopped. I think, if we can isolate him in the Inn, it would be easier. You know it might be a good idea if Doris was in the lounge when they came back. She might be able to separate Lisa from Harry. Do you think she would?"

"Of course. I'll call her. I think she'll want to be there to comfort Lisa." Charles picked up the phone.

They had misjudged. Instead of using the main entrance, Harry parked next to the side entrance for employees that was near his office. Inside the narrow hallway he saw the back of Sergeant Rodgers standing outside his office door. A surprised Harry spontaneously called out. "Sergeant!"

The sergeant who was facing toward the lounge area, where they expected him to come from, was startled. He turned and said. "Lieutenant, Harry's here"

Manny moved quickly to the door. "Harry you are under arrest for the murder of Louisa Perez. You have the right to…"

Lisa screamed. "Oh my God! No, no, it can't be."

In that instant she moved slightly in front of Harry who grabbed her arm and shoved her toward Manny and the Sergeant. The hallway was narrow and this provided a perfect block, especially when Manny and the sergeant instinctively both reached out for the falling Lisa.

Harry bolted out the side door, down the path, and into his car. The car, in reverse, lurched out of the parking space, throwing a spray of gravel into the air. The darkness and vegetation blocked Sergeant Rodgers's view as he came out of the door. Instinctively his weapon was in his hand and aimed. "Halt or I'll shoot! Harry halt! Stop the car!"

From behind him he heard Manny shout. "Don't fire Steve! It's too risky. We'll get him. Head for the cruiser." Hearing the door slam behind him, he said, "Charles head for the cruiser."

Sergeant Rodgers was behind the wheel and Manny and Charles sat in the back of the cruiser as it sped down the dirt road toward the main road. Sergeant Rodgers made the call to other cruisers. "Black, late model, Toyota SUV, Arizona plate IRONDR. Approach with caution."

Manny whose eyes were riveted on the road in front of the cruiser, said. "Tell that cruiser in front of us to pull in behind. Tell everyone, if they contain him, not to approach him until we get there." Then looking at Charles continued. "He knows us. Maybe we can calm him down."

Looking somber, Charles said. "That reaction was a complete surprise to me. I expected denial, or maybe outrage, but to bolt like that. What could he expect to accomplish? What's he thinking?"

"He's not. Desperate people usually don't." And then addressing Sergeant Rodgers, "It would be good if we stop him from going into the city. Block off Oracle road."

Before the Sergeant could issue this instruction, another officer's voice came over the radio, "Suspect just turned right on Ina. He's driving madly. He almost hit two cars going through the light to make the turn."

A look of concern crossed Manny's face. "Put the word out to wait till he's in a less populated area before attempting to contain him. We don't want to make a high-speed chase out this. We've got time."

The traffic was inhibiting Harry's progress, but not the cruisers with their sirens on and lights flashing.

Sergeant Rodgers said, "There he is. He's in front of us lieutenant, in the passing lane."

"OK, let's go easy now; he's probably going to I10. Block both north and south entrances to I10. That would be a good place to contain him."

"Lieutenant! We've a situation up ahead, at the railroad crossing; barriers are down, traffic piling up."

Manny was leaning forward as close as he could get to the windshield. "I don't like doing it, but we'll have to take him. Hopefully he will surrender without incident."

"My God!" Charles blurted out, "He's swung out, going around the cars and the barrier."

Two powerful blasts, followed by a long one, billowed a warning from the train. Sparks flew up from the wheels as the brakes locked. The screeching sound of metal on metal pierced the ears of those who waited at the crossing.

Along with the motorists, the three in the cruiser watched a man gamble his life. Those watching the impact of the train and the car knew the skills of the Paramedics would not have to be tested. When the car was struck, pieces of metal and glass flew into the air as the car was dragged down the track. The chase was over.

Charles asked, "Was that a gamblers choice or suicide?"

"A real gambler wouldn't bet on those odds," Manny said, "I think it was suicide."

"It had to be. He couldn't have missed seeing how close the train was. He didn't have a chance." Having said that, Sergeant Rodgers maneuvered the cruiser as close as he could to the stopped train and the demolished SUV. The emergency work and long night of investigation had begun for officers and railroad employees, but for Manny it was wrap up time for a murder investigation.

On the way back to the Inn the three of them sat quietly, for the most part. There was some radio communication going on. Because of this Manny sat in the front seat next to Sergeant Rodgers. Charles sat in the back seat and pondered over the futility of it all. He had endangered all those people and took his own life. After all this was over, he wanted to learn more about Harry's life. He knew things like this just didn't happen. It took years of circumventing the rules of society to lead to such desperation. Maybe sometime in the future he would talk to Lisa about it. His thoughts were interrupted when Manny said to no one in particular. "Now for the tough part of the job."

Charles sat at the desk in Harry's office waiting for Manny to break the news to Lisa. He knew Doris was still with her and that that would be a comfort to her, at least until a relative could be contacted. Manny's notebook was on the desk along with the bank bag, with which they never confronted Harry. Putting back on his latex gloves, he picked up the bag and took out the contents. The question of motive came to mind as he looked at the money and then at the small white ticket. A chill went through his body followed by a shiver. My God! Could it be possible?

Manny entered the office. When he saw Charles's face staring at the desktop, without acknowledging his presence, he said. “Charles what’s wrong? You seem to be deep in thought.”

“Am I ever? All this time we either didn’t have a motive, or when we found what could have been one, the small amount of money, it didn’t make sense.”

“And now you know something?” Manny said.

“I have a theory about what happened. It just came to me while I was waiting for you and looking at the contents of the bag. It can be proven with one phone call, but first let me give you my idea of what happened.”

“When he went to Louisa’s, about eight thirty, he found her distraught. Feeling abandoned by Carlos and guilty over her stealing, she confessed everything and gave the moneybag to Harry. He came back here and went through the bag as he sat at his desk. He probably put the contents on his desk and checked the marked bills. Now from that time to ten twenty I don’t have any idea what he did, but at ten twenty I think he had the TV on. He wanted to check his lottery tickets. He took down the number. Four lottery tickets were found in the wastebasket under the desk. All of them for Saturday’s drawing. None of them checked out. Then he picked up the one that was in the bag. It did.”

“If it is the winning number, how can you prove it was not one of his?” Asked Manny.

“If it is the winner, the date, time, and place it was purchased will be known.”

“And?” Probed Manny.

“And, I have the receipt from the Circle K where I bought it.”

“It makes sense that it wasn’t one of his, if it was one of his, nobody would have been murdered.” Manny said. Then he picked up the phone and the ticket. “It’s time to find out.”

His theory about to be tested, Charles felt a rush of excitement through his body. Not only the personal satisfaction of resolving the motive question, but he could be a millionaire.

"Hello, this is Lieutenant Manny Gomez, Pima County Sheriff's Department, would you check this number out. Yes, that's it. Saturday night's drawing. A slight smile appeared on Manny's face as he said, "Thank you." He replaced the phone, paused, and said. "You're not only a clever man, but a rich one."

"Did they mention the jackpot?"

"One million two hundred thousand dollars."

Charles wanted to rush to Doris and tell her, but first there were questions. He said, "How do I go about claiming the money, considering the ticket is evidence."

"There's not going to be a trial. I think a copy of the ticket and your receipt will be sufficient for the record. I'll run it by legal when I get back to the office, if there are no problems, you can claim it tomorrow. I'll give you a call as soon as I find out."

"Thank you, Manny."

Charles closed he door of the room and not seeing Doris, he called out, "Doris!"

Doris stood up from her chair and said. "I'm on the patio. Oh! I'm so glad you're back. Lisa is so grieved, it's one thing to lose somebody, but in such a tragic manner. Harry's sister is coming to help her with the funeral arrangements. I told her we would stay to help."

Unable to contain himself any longer, Charles walked over to her and placed his arms on her shoulders. "We're millionaires!"

"What! What're you talking about?"

"The lottery ticket, the ticket I lost. Louisa stole it. Harry took the moneybag back to his office and found out it was a winner. It was the motive."

Doris, dumfounded and shaken, hugged Charles. As the tears flowed she said. "It's so wonderful for us, but do you think we can help Lisa?"

"Of course. It's not something we haven't talked about. We both liked the idea of owning an Inn. I think she's a great manager. We could buy it and have her manage it, or invest money in it."

"I can't wait to tell her. It won't help her grief, but it will lift a heavy burden off her shoulders. When do we get the money?"

"The lottery ticket is actually evidence, so Manny is checking it out with the legal department. He said he would call me in the morning."

Charles was on the patio having his second cup of coffee. He and Doris had finished breakfast. She had gone to check on Lisa and he was doing what one is supposed to do on vacation, relaxing. Not expecting to hear from Manny so early, he was surprised to see and hear him say, "Good morning, millionaire!"

"Only on paper at this point. I'm surprised to see you. I expected a call."

Manny sat down and placed the ticket on the table in front of Charles. "You know out here, when you win the lottery you buy breakfast."

"Fair enough, but with your appetite you'd have to be the big winner to pay for it."

"Well, I'll go easy on you since you haven't got the money yet. That's not the only reason I came over. I wanted to thank you for a great piece of work and the captain, who was impressed by your work, sends his congratulations. We were talking and we both thought it would be great if you could give one of your courses here. I know I'd like to take one."

Charles smiled and said, "I think you already have."

---The End---

TRUTH BE TOLD

By A. C. Boyan

Charles finished his eggs and sipped his coffee. His wife Doris watered the plants along the patio rail. They both enjoyed having their breakfast on the patio. The view was serene. The mountains served as a backdrop and a sandy wash with cottonwood trees bordering it were in the foreground

"It's hard to believe the changes in just one year." Charles said.

"It worked out well didn't it?" Doris and Charles Knowles were retired and moved from Seattle to the Iron Door Inn.

"Yes, it did, but we did our homework, visiting different parts of the country."

Doris set down the watering can and went to the table to finish her coffee. "But I never expected to be living in an Inn. It's perfect."

Lisa Wright, the owner of the Inn accepted their offer to buy two rooms at the Inn in a condominium arrangement. They had become friends of hers during past visits, searching for a retirement location. Doris, whose pleasant, small featured face that always seemed on the edge of a smile, said, "Speaking of changes, I'm having a hard time adjusting to your beardless face."

"Being a professor all those years, I think it went with the occupation. I don't really know why I shaved it. Maybe it was the change of coming from the cold, raw Seattle climate to this dry, warm, desert climate. I don't know. But it does feel good." After he finished his coffee he asked, "What are your plans for today?"

"I'm going to be helping in the kitchen, but this time doing something more to my liking. I am going to be working with the chef. Lisa wants me to show him a couple of my recipes." This was one of the things Doris loved about having retired to the Inn. There were so many areas she could work and help by filling in, at the front desk, gardening, the kitchen, either when someone didn't show up, or they became very busy. "How about you?"

"I'm going to take a hike with Will. He loves to walk in the canyon, but he's uncomfortable doing it alone. I tell him all about the flora and fauna and he does retain some of the names, especially the birds. He gets very excited when he can name a flower or bird. He repeats it over and over and breaks out in a big smile."

"Are you taking a lunch?'

"Yes."

"OK, have fun."

William Smith came to the Inn about six months ago and worked as a kitchen helper. When Charles first met Will, he told him he knew Bill was also a nickname for William but that he preferred Will. He was friendly, honest, and a good worker. Charles liked Will and took an interest in him; his background in psychology played a part in his interest. They spent time playing checkers in the lounge or taking hikes in the canyon and wash. Will liked to take back a rock, flower, or some other treasure they had found on the hike for his collection. He kept his collection in his room in the big building next to the Inn. There were a few rooms in this building, called the maintenance building, for employees. It was a small room with a bed, a pine chest of drawers, a mirror in a pine frame hung above this, and a bookcase. Nothing was out of place. The bookcase with five shelves sat in the corner of the room. It was here that he kept his collection. Not only did it hold his nature collection but all the other things he liked to collect as well. These consisted of odds and ends he found in his daily routine, from trashcans, and the dumpster. These he shared with anyone he thought might need them.

Will was twenty-five, six feet tall, broad shouldered, no neck, short dark hair, and a serious face that could turn into a disarming smile. He walked in a determined manner and held his head tilted back. Suddenly he shouted, "There's one! There's one! Over there! The red one."

He ran off the canyon trail toward the red one and lost his footing on the loose rock and slid on his backside. Charles rushed over to help him and realized he was all right when he quickly got up and straightened his baseball cap, although it never did seem to be straight. "Did you see it? The red one. Did you see it?"

"Yes, that's a Cardinal."

"Yes, the Cardinal. I've got it on my list. Right Charles?"

"Yes, that's on your list. Now when bird watching, you have to move very slowly and be very quiet so you can get a longer look at the bird." Charles said, but thought; I can't remember when I've had so much fun bird watching.

"Yes, that's right. You have to be patient. It's very serious business. Maybe we'll see an owl. They have big eyes. I'd like that."

This pleased Charles. It meant that Will was looking at the bird book he had given him. "You only see them at night."

Eyes wide, Will jerked his head. "At night?" he said. "How can you see them at night?"

"Usually you hear them hooting and then you use a flashlight to find them."

"I'm going to get a flashlight and, when I hear them hoot, I'll find them."

After he spotted a few more birds and collected some wildflowers, they had lunch on an outcropping that overlooked the canyon. From here they could admire the giant saguaro cactus and desert vegetation all the way down to the river below.

Charles broke the companionable silence of their lunch break. "Is that a new watch?"

Will moved it closer for Charles's observation. "Yes it is. I saved up for it. It's a very special watch."

"It looks it. Where did you get it?

"Wal-Mart. It has a big clock and at night it lights up. It's very important to be on time for work. Very important."

Later that afternoon, Will said, "We have to go back now, so I won't be late for work."

"Oh! This is Monday. I thought you were off on Monday and Tuesday."

"Yes, I'm off at the Inn, but I help at the stables."

Charles knew he went to the stables on his time off but didn't know he was working there. "What kind of work do you do there?"

"I help clean the stables, empty the trash, and sometimes walk and feed the horses. It's very important. I don't always work though. Laura's teaching me to ride and someday she's going to take me on a trail ride."

"They seem to be very kind people." Charles said.

"They are very nice. They are very nice people, most of them."

They had reached the back of the Inn. Charles thought, I'll follow up on that later.

The Trail Dust Stables was an old ranch that was modernized for boarding horses and giving trail rides. The layout of the property was in the shape of a U. The ranch house was a two-storied building with a covered porch on three sides. A small addition was made on one side with an office and a parking area to accommodate customers.

The front of the house over looked the corral that had a large barn building on each side. Looking out from the ranch house porch, the building on the right was the newer one for boarding horses. It was a long building and each of the stalls could be accessed from the outside. The overhanging barn roof ran the length of the building and covered this open area. The half doors to the stalls were left opened. Most of the horses usually had their heads sticking out to socialize.

The building on the left was also a long large building, but older. There were large double doors on each end of the building. An aisle, big enough to drive a wagon through, ran from the front to the back. On each side of this were stalls for the ranch horses and a large tack room.

After an early evening meal, Will took the path along the wash leading to the Trail Dust Stables. When he got there, the late afternoon trail ride had just returned. Dust hung over the corral as the ten riders rode in and dismounted. The customers hitched their mounts to the rail and left. Laura Mendez, an employee at the ranch, took off the first saddle and saw Will. "Hi Will, you're just in time to help put away the saddles."

Just then another voice came from the other side of one of the horses. "Hey Will, get on the other side and when I undo the belts you carry the saddle to the rack wagon." It was the voice of Larry Coleman, a part time employee who was a student at the University of Arizona.

"Don't do it Will. He's just trying to get you to do all the work," Laura said.

"I won't Laura. I'll do my own. He's not a nice person." It wasn't the first time Larry had played a joke on Will or got him to do his work.

With a display of mocked sadness, Larry said, "Oh, you hurt my feelings."

A deep voice came from a tall lanky man named Rusty Johnson. "I'll hurt your ass if you don't stop playing around. Let's get this tack away; I don't want to be here all night." Rusty was thirty-five, the wrangler, and his weather beaten, gaunt face was testimony to years spent working on a ranch. Heeding this advice, Larry became a team player in removing the saddles.

Two other employees met the group when they entered the barn with the saddle wagon. Raul and Pam had just finished mucking out the stalls for the evening. Laura joined them as they went out to lead the horses in. Will, Larry, and Rusty unloaded the wagon contents to the tack room.

"Larry, you check the stalls for food and water. Will, you can sweep out the floor." Rusty said, and left the barn.

Laura, Pam, and Raul led the horses into their stalls, then removed and stored the bridles in the tack room. Their work finished, Raul and Pam left the barn. Laura stayed behind, as she usually did, to check out her favorite horse. This was Gallant, the one she used for trail rides and when she was teaching. She petted him and gave him his nightly treat.

Will was at the far end of the barn sweeping and shoveling droppings into the wheelbarrow. "Larry called out, "Hey Will, you missed some droppings in front of Fury's stall."

"I see it. I see it. I'm not blind." Fury was a wild, one-man horse. That man was Rusty. There was a bright red sign on the stall that read DANGER KEEP OUT. Rusty had given instructions to everyone to stay away from that horse.

Larry tauntingly said, "Then why don't you pick it up? You afraid?"

The fact of the matter was that Fury intimidated Will, all of them were. And he had ignored the droppings because they were so close to the stall. Now he approached with extreme caution, shovel in hand. As he lowered the shovel to pick up the droppings, Larry reached over from the next stall and poked Fury with the handle of a shavings fork. Fury in a fit of rage lowered his head and front shoulders and raised his hind end battering the stall gate with his hooves.

Will bolted upright and dropped the shovel in panic. When he looked up he saw Larry in the next stall ready to repeat the assault. His fear turned to anger. He shouted, "Stop, stop, that's cruel." His muscles seemed to expand and made him look larger in his charge toward Larry. Terror filled Larry's eyes and he turned to face Will and tried to use the handle of the shavings fork, which was in both hands, to fend off Will. Will, in one simple movement grabbed the handle and threw Larry out of the stall. The shavings fork went one way and Larry landed on the floor.

"What the hell's the matter with you? You crazy?"

"You're mean and cruel. I'm going to take you to Rusty. You'll be punished for that. That's very wrong. Very wrong."

Larry got up and made a futile attempt to defend himself. With fire in his eyes, Will threw a hammerlock on him and dragged him the length of the barn with no more trouble than carrying a bag of feed.

His eyes bulged and Larry screamed, "Put me down! You're crazy! Help, he's killing me!"

Laura heard the commotion and ran out of Gallant's stall. "What's going on? Will put him down. What are you doing?'

"I'm taking him to Rusty. He's cruel to the horses. He's not a nice person."

Rusty had run up to the barn entrance and said in a deep penetrating voice. "What the hell are you doing Will? Put him down. Now!"

Will let go of a very relieved Larry and explained. "I was bringing him to you. He was poking Fury. He's mean. He should be punished."

"OK, just relax. Call it a night. I'll take care of this." Rusty motioned to Larry in the direction of the barn and they both walked back into the barn.

Laura took Will by the arm. "Are you OK?'

"I'm OK."

"Let's go get a snack."

"Snacks are good. I'm going to have Pepsi and Fritos."

Tuesday morning Raul and Pam were doing the morning mucking out of the stables at the far end of the barn. Pam approached Gallant's stall, which was two away from Fury's, and stopped cold in her tracks. An arm stuck up from under Fury's gate. She moved closer to confirm it was. She screamed and ran out of the barn to the office.

After verifying the gruesome discovery, Rusty called the Pima County Sheriff's Department and sat by the barn door and waited for the police to arrive. It wasn't long. The cruiser raised dust as it passed the office and pulled up in front of the barn.

Rusty stood up and greeted the officers as they walked up the barn ramp. The first one was Lieutenant Detective Manny Gomez. "Sounds like you've got a problem Rusty."

"We sure do."

Manny turned to the other officer and said. "This is Sergeant Steve Rodgers."

Rusty extended his hand. "Howdy."

Manny was 33 years old and had worked eleven years for the Sheriff's Department. He stood 5' 11" and had a well-developed upper body. After asking and being informed that the owners of the stables, Rachel and Ernest Ortega, were on vacation, he asked, "Where's the body?"

Rusty pushed the barn door opened and said. "At the far end of the barn. Fury's stall."

They walked in silence through to the far end of the barn. When they reached the stall Manny asked, "Is this how you found it?"

"No, the gate was closed I had to open it to see the body. Fury was very jumpy so I move him to another stall."

"Why the sign on the gate?" Manny inquired.

"Fury is very temperamental. Anything can set him off. He was mistreated and badly neglected when he was young, so I adopted him and brought him here. I take care of him and no one is allowed to go near him."

"Why would Larry go near the stall? Manny asked.

"He was mean to him. I had to take him aside just last night and tell him if he didn't stop, I'd have to fire him."

"Last night?" Manny said, "What happened?"

Rusty went over the events of the night before. He appeared uncomfortable, either from his taciturn nature, or being questioned by the police.

A member of the Forensic Unit, who called out to Manny, interrupted the questioning. "Lieutenant, any special instructions?"

"Yes, the horse has been moved to that other stall, check him out. He may have to be tranquillized first. His name is Fury and he has a bad disposition."

Manny turned to Rusty and said. "Where can we locate this Will Smith?"

"At the Iron Door Inn." Then with unexpected verbiage Rusty continued. "He works there. He likes horses, so he comes over here. He picks up extra money doing chores and Laura gives him riding lessons."

"After you had your talk with Larry what did he do?"

Rusty shrugged. "He apologized. Said he couldn't afford to lose his job. He needed the money for school and he wouldn't do it again. I said I'd give him one more chance and he left."

"What do we have Lieutenant?" The voice came from behind Manny.

"Oh, hi Fred." After greeting Fred, he said to Rusty, "That's it for now. If I have any more questions I'll contact you."

Turning back to Fred, he said, "There are no eyewitnesses, but the horse has a violent history and the victim was known to taunt him. It looks like he was kicked to death. The body is in his stall. Fury, the horse's name, was moved over there."

"That must have taken a lot of guts. Who moved him?"

"Rusty. It's a one-man horse." Manny gave a brief account of Fury's history.

Fred had knelt down next to the body and started his examination. Having had a good working relationship with Fred, Manny waited in silence until the appropriate time and then asked. "What's your first call"?

"He has two bad head wounds; one on the side and one on the back. I'd say trauma to the head did him in." Fred said.

One of the forensic unit's members, George, a studious looking young man with a stubby beard, addressed Manny. "Lieutenant, we found blood samples on the wood shavings in the empty stall next to Fury's. It could have traveled that far, but there are obstructions in the trajectory path. Of course, it might not be a blood match. We'll check it out. I thought it might be something you'd want to know up front."

Both men walked to the area and George pointed it out. Manny squatted down and could see the stained wood shavings. "Thanks George. That could broaden the investigation."

Manny enquired at the Iron Door Inn and found out that it was Will's day off and that he could be found over at the Trail Dust Stables on his days off. He then asked if Charles was around. He had met Charles on a previous investigation at the Inn, and when he learned of his work with the Seattle Police Department, he accepted Charles' offer to help. The clerk said that he was out in the maintenance building.

"Hi Charles, this is a nice workshop you set up here," Manny said and nodded his head in approval.

Charles looked up from his table saw and replied. “Oh, hi Manny. He turned off the table saw and lifted his safety glasses. “I put up two walls to section it off from the maintenance work area, added the workbenches and then the fluorescent lighting.”

Manny reached up and opened one of the cabinets. “Great storage space,” he said. “That’s what I need. My shop is so cluttered I can’t find anything.”

Charles thought that statement coming from Manny was incongruous. With a man like Manny who was so meticulous about his dress, starched long sleeve white shirt, sharply creased black pants, and polished shoes, there could be only one reason.

Charles said, “Manny, with the demands of your job, I don’t see how you could find much time to even work in your shop. Maybe when you retire you can set it up the way you want. What brings you here?”

“It’s business. A young employee was killed at the Trail Dust Stables.”

“An accident? Do you have time to talk about it? Good let’s go in the employee lunch room and have a coffee.”

The employee lunch and break area was set up in the middle of the maintenance building. It was equipped with evaporative cooling, tables and chairs, soda and coffee machines. The two men took their coffee to the far end of the room, not wanting to be overheard. Charles reopened the conversation. “If it happened at the Trail Dust, what brings you here?”

“I was told about an incident involving a Will Smith and the victim last night. I came over but was informed he was over at the Trail dust. Do you know him?”

“Yes. I’ve become friends with him. He came here about six months ago. What kind of incident?”

Manny went on to explain the incident and then asked. “Are you familiar with his condition?’

"As I understand it, his mental limitations were caused as a result of a brain operation when he was young. I've spent a lot of time with him; hiking, playing games, and I've never seen him violent. Excited, yes. That's not to say he couldn't be, he has strong convictions."

Manny stood up and went over to the sandwich machine. "Ever try these? I think I'll eat while I can."

"The ham and cheese is good." While Manny did this, Charles thought through the facts. He had his next question but waited for Manny to open up his sandwich. "First, we have a victim found dead in a stall with a wild horse he has been known to provoke. Second, you learned of an employee, Will, who had a confrontation with the victim the night before over his meanness to the horse. Now the forensic unit hasn't had time to do a report yet, but I sense, Manny that you have some preliminary evidence that might suggest the horse was not the perpetrator. Do you?"

"Right, one of the forensic team showed me what looked like a blood stain in the adjacent stall next to the stall where the victim was found. It was a small amount and could have traveled there if it wasn't for the five foot partition wall and a corner post."

"Which presents a possibility that he was killed and moved to Fury's stall to make it look like an accident." Both men sat quietly for a moment and Charles added, "If that was the case, there would have been more blood-stained shavings which means somebody cleaned up."

"Also, because of the confrontation with Will last night, it makes him a suspect. So, I'm going to go find Will and question him." Manny said.

Charles was saddened by the thought of Will being questioned and the fact he could be involved. "Even if he did do this in an act of violence, I can't imagine him covering up and in such a manner as to implicate a horse he took action to protect before the crime."

"Good point."

"Will doesn't have any close relatives that I know of and I'm concerned how he is going to take the questioning. Would it be alright if I came along?" Charles asked.

A broad smile crossed Manny's face. "Who's closer to the circumstance or better qualified? You preempted my asking."

Will ambled in as Charles and Manny got up to leave. Charles called out, "Hi Will."

When Will saw Charles, his face lit up. "Hi Charles."

"I thought you were over at the Trail Dust," Charles said.

"Came back for lunch. The sandwiches are better here. I'm going back at two thirty for riding lessons with Laura."

"Will, this is a friend of mine, Manny Gomez, he's a detective with the Pima County Sheriff's Department."

Manny offered his hand. "Hi Will."

"Hi. I like your cowboy hat. It's like Rusty's except his is black. I'm going to get one, and boots for riding."

"Will, if it's alright with you, I'd like to buy you lunch and we could sit together." Charles asked.

"Good, I'd like that."

As the three of them sat at the table, Charles and Manny, with snacks and drinks, watched Will methodically set out his lunch in front of him. He first spread a napkin and placed his sandwich on it. He then opened up packages of mustard, ketchup, relish and mayonnaise, and squeezed each one on his sandwich. As he did this, his eyes shifted back and forth at Manny, especially at the 9mm Beretta holstered on Manny's hip.

Charles felt very comfortable with the way this was going. He thought it would have been so much more intimidating for Will if Manny had to question him alone, or if he had to be taken to the police station to be questioned. Charles asked, “Will, do you know what happened at the Trail Dust?”

“Yes, Laura and Pam told me. Pam found the body, she’s very upset.”

Manny in a flat tone and direct manner said, “Were you very upset?”

“Yes, it’s very sad, but, truth be told, he was mean to Fury and got punished. He was a mean person.”

Manny recorded this statement in his notebook and said to Charles. “I’ll send you a copy of all the notes.”

“Will, when you mentioned to me that they all weren’t nice people at the Trail Dust, to whom were you referring?” Charles said.

“Larry, he was always playing jokes on me. Laura told me not to pay attention to him. Sometimes she told me when he was doing it. He didn’t like it and told her to mind her own business.”

“What happened last night?” Manny asked.

“He poked Fury when I was next to his stall picking up droppings. He wanted to scare me.”

Manny waited for Will to finish his cheese and peanut butter crackers and continued. “What did you do then?”

“I wrestled him and brought him to Rusty.”

“What did you do after that?”

“Laura and I had a snack and then I went back to my room.”

“What time was that Will?” Charles asked.

“I don’t know. I lost my watch when I wrestled with Larry. I had to go back and get it. It’s broken. I’ll have to take it back to Wal-Mart.”

Both men perked up and looked at each other. Manny in his kind demeanor explained. “When something is found at an accident scene, it's called evidence. We have to take that watch, but I tell you what, we'll get you a new one. Where is the watch?"

"It's in my room."

The two men stood outside Will's room waiting for him to retrieve the watch.

"What do you make of it?" Charles asked.

"Not Good. The picture I'm getting puts him back at the crime scene. What if Larry found the watch and teased Will with it when he came back. That would be like waving a steak in front of a hungry lion."

Charles knew this was a logical scenario and had a sinking feeling. "What are you going to do?" The question went unanswered when Will returned with the watch.

In the parking lot, Manny answered. "I'm going to wait for the Forensic report and conduct some more interviews. I'll have Steve drop off the notes on what we have including any forensic info."

"Thanks."

"Will's going to need all the help he can get." Manny said.

And the way the evidence is developing, Charles thought, I'm going to need all the time I can get before they make an arrest.

That evening at dinner, Charles sat with Doris and Lisa. It was Italian night on the patio and Charles and Doris enjoyed these theme evenings. It was a warm night and the patio was colorfully decorated and well lit. The back of the Inn was terraced; the patio was on the first level and the swimming pool was on the lower level. From here you could see the Mesquite trees bordering the Cañada Del Oro wash.

"What happened at the stables?" Doris didn't wait for an answer. "I understand there was a terrible accident."

Lisa added, "I've been friends with the Ortegas for years, they're owners of the Trail Dust, and they called from San Diego and asked if I would look after things at the Trail Dust. I heard Manny came looking for you."

They both expressed a wide-eyed look of anticipation and Charles paused with knife and fork in hand over his spaghetti and meatballs and attempted to satisfy their curiosity. "Yes, a young man name Larry Coleman died from injuries caused by a disturbed horse named Fury. Of course, that's just the preliminary findings." He started to eat while the next questions were formulated.

"I knew Larry; he was a U of A student. He worked part time. Why was Manny looking for you?" Lisa asked.

"You said preliminary findings," Doris said, "have you or Manny come up with any secondary findings? Especially ones that would put you in a melancholy mood."

Charles thought–bulls' eye–and said with uncommon difficulty, "Manny was actually looking for Will. He caught up with me in the workshop and we went to the lunch area." He then went on to explain the general scenario that Manny came up with and their subsequent interview with Will.

Both women were flabbergasted. Doris said with sympathy in her eyes, "That's terrible. Is there anything you can do to help?"

"I'm going to try."

Back in their apartment, Charles sat at his oak desk under a large window with a view of the mountains. The desk was a three-part unit that fit in the corner. The corner section holding his computer, and the two adjoining units were good size desks with file drawers. On his way back to the room, the clerk had given him the notes that were dropped off by Sergeant Rodgers and these were spread on the desk along side an opened notebook.

Doris sat in an armchair with her latest cooking magazine. “I’ve a feeling you’re going to be up late.”

As he leaned back and played with his pen, Charles replied. “It’s critical that I organize a plan. There’s not much time. When the lab report comes in, they’re going to arrest Will, or certainly will question him more. I hope I can come up with something to delay that.”

“Who will you start with?”

“What’s the first question that came to you?” Charles turned in his chair and looked at Doris.

“The shock of it raised many questions, but thinking it through, one stands out. Why did Larry go back there?”

“Yes, why?” Charles turned back to his notebook and began outlining his plan as he spoke to Doris. “I am going to have to start the interview with Larry, a person who can’t answer my questions.”

“How are you going to do that?”

“I’m going to find out about him through those who knew him”

“I’d like to start with Lisa at breakfast. I’m sure she could provide good background information and give me the names of the employees.”

“I’ll call her and ask her to join us for breakfast,” Doris said.

When everyone had their coffee, and waited to be served breakfast, Charles got down to business. “Lisa, did you know Larry?”

“Just casually, I saw him when I went over to go on trail rides, or when I visited the Ortegas.”

Charles placed his notebook on the table and asked. “Did you learn anything about his background? His personality?”

"I did get the impression he was arrogant."

Breakfast was served, but the questions continued. "Why?"

"By the way he acted toward the other employees," Lisa said.

"How so?"

"Well, the only way I can explain it is it was like a spoiled rich kid going to college and working along side the peasants."

"Not a pretty picture." Doris said.

Charles thought as he sat in silence and wrote the last comments in his notebook, was he a spoiled rich kid, or a poor kid acting to cover up his insecurity? Charles excused himself and left while Lisa and Doris had another coffee.

He drove over to the Trail Dust and parked next to the office. Rusty was in the office, which was an addition to the ranch house, Charles explained to him that he was assisting the Pima County Sheriff's Department with their interviewing process and would like to go over the events of the tragic accident. They were both familiar with each other because of occasional walks that Charles took to look at the horses.

The use of the wording, interviewing process, instead of investigation, seemed to mollify Rusty. In a soft tone he said, "I didn't know you worked for the PCSD."

"Oh, occasionally I help out. They have quite a work load." And then when he saw the puzzled looked on Rusty's face, continued, "I used to do that in Seattle."

"What do you want to know?" Rusty opened up a section of the counter top and nodded in the direction of a desk with two chairs.

"Why would Larry go near the stall, or into it?"

"Fury was a mean horse. Larry liked to tease him."

"When someone does this they are showing off, or they do it to scare someone. Why do you think he would do this when he was alone with fury and late at night?" Charles asked.

"Maybe he got his kicks out of it."

Charles didn't expect an answer to this question but wanted to see his reaction to it.

There was the possibility Rusty might have seen Larry do it in the past. Charles thought it was time to ask questions he should be able to answer. "How long have you had Fury?"

"About five years." Rusty got up and asked, "Like some coffee?"

"Sure." When Rusty brought the coffee over and set it on the desk, Charles sipped it and said, "Thanks, strong but good."

Rusty, with a chuckle, said, "Yeah, I use the left over to peel paint."

"Where did Fury come from?"

"The old Buena Vista Ranch, about five miles from here. I did some work for them and, when I saw the condition of the horse, I asked if I could buy it. They agreed so I bartered some work for him."

"I better write some of this down, or I'll forget it. It's probably not important," Charles said, "but if I don't write it down, later I'll think I missed something." Expecting a more hostile interview, Charles was surprised at Rusty's relaxed attitude.

"I know how it is. I forget things all the time." Rusty said.

"Did Fury have any stable vices? You know, cribbing, biting, nervousness."

Rusty leaned back and put his boots on the desk. "No, he just doesn't like strangers. He gets hyper active and you don't know what he's going to do. I've seen him kick down the stall gate."

"Where can I find the other employees?"

Both men stood up. Rusty lifted his black cowboy hat and readjusted it on his head. “Pam and Raul are mucking out the stalls. Laura’s grooming Gallant in the corral.”

“Thanks, Rusty, I’ll talk to you later.”

“I hope they don’t put Fury down. He had no business being near him. It was posted.”

As he walked through the barn, on the way to Fury’s stall, the pungent smells of leather, manure, and straw, brought back childhood memories of his summer visits to a farm. He expected to see Raul and Pam, but he didn’t. It was during those farm visits that he became familiar with all the farm animals. Horses were his favorites and looked even bigger and were more intimidating to a young boy, but he bonded to the horses and was very comfortable around them. So it was now, as he approached this horse with a bad reputation for meanness.

He made the approach through the adjacent stall with the five-foot wood stall partition separating him. There was enough room between the wood boards that enabled him to raise himself up and lean in closer to Fury’s head.

Fury snorted a few times and shifted in the stall. Charles started the interview. “How you doing boy? Here, look at you; you’re a good-looking horse. You got yourself in a lot of trouble. Anything you want to tell me?”

This was said in a soft, calming tone. He reached over and stroked him gently as he said. “Good boy, good boy.” Fury’s original nervousness dissipated.

Charles withdrew the stroking arm and balanced himself while the other hand reached in his pocket for the ultimate peace offering, sugar cubes.

He took a deep breath as he positioned the offering so Fury could reach it. At this point, he didn’t see any signs of erratic behavior, but it could go either way.

Fury spoke for the first time. He bobbed his head, stretched his neck, and accepted the offering with friendly excitement.

Charles mustered up his courage for the next test. He walked to Fury's stall gate and opened it. Staying as far away from Fury's rear end as he could, he cautiously walked to the front of the stall, and talked in a soft tone all the way. More treats were offered and happily accepted.

The interview was over and Charles told Fury he believed him, but he didn't like the alternative. Then his cell phone rang.

"Hi Manny. I'm at the crime scene. Yeah, I got an early start. Things are moving right along. I already talked to Lisa, Rusty, and Fury."

"Oh, I am always learning something new about you Charles. You talk to horses."

"Yes, and I believe him."

"Well, that's not unusual for him to say he's innocent, is it Charles? Being a policeman, I hear the perpetrators say that all the time."

Charles explained, "I am familiar with horses and the thing I learned is that they don't lie. He didn't show any abnormal behavior towards me. I am going to look into it further. He has a bad reputation and I want to know how he got it."

"I called to give you the lab results. The blood samples in the adjacent stall match Larry Coleman's. You're right about Fury. He's off the hook.'

On the one hand, Charles was relieved, on the other, he knew where the hook was going, but had to ask. "Who's on the hook?"

"Everything points to Will. I'm putting it all together now, and then I'm going to bring him in for questioning and possibly arrest."

"Is there anything you can do to delay it? I'm going to need some time, at least the rest of the afternoon."

"He's not going anywhere and I've got a lot of paper work to do. Give me a call if you come up with anything significant that might help me justify the delay. Good luck Charles."

Charles replaced his phone and walked to the other end of the barn. When he reached the barn door, Pam and Raul came in. They were familiar with each other on a first name basis. Due to the nature of the business at hand, Charles made a formal introduction and gave the same explanation he gave to Rusty. Both were friendly and Pam told her story of discovery, purging herself of a nightmarish experience. All the time Raul sympathetically stared at her.

When she was finished, Charles asked, "How long has the adjacent stall been empty?"

It was Raul's turn, "For a long time. It's not needed and the horses used for trail rides are placed closer to the barn entrance, which is near the corral where they are lined up for the guests."

Charles, remembering his childhood farm visits, asked, "I noticed you use woodchips instead of straw in the stalls, is there any advantage?"

Raul answered, "It doesn't move around as much as straw when the horses bed down."

Pam added, "It's easier to keep clean. It was Rusty's idea. He changed over shortly after he came here."

"How often do you muck it out?"

Pam said, "Twice a day." Raul nodded in agreement.

"How about the empty stall next to Fury's; when was that last mucked out?" Charles asked.

The answers that came from both were; I don't know and a long time ago.

Charles knew he was holding them from doing their work. So he asked his last question. "Who mucks out Fury's stall?"

"Rusty, he's the only one allowed to go near Fury," Pam said.

Raul said, "That's a mean horse. He was mistreated when he was young. Rusty saved him from the glue factory."

This prompted one more question. "Other than the times he was taunted, did either of you ever see him act wild."

They both looked at each other and said, "No."

Charles thanked them and left the barn. He sat on a tree stump just outside the barn and went over his notes. When he looked up, he saw his next interview in the corral, Laura.

Laura was grooming Gallant when Charles said, "Good morning Laura." He was more familiar with her than the others. He had talked to her a couple of times when he visited.

"Good morning Charles. Out for a walk?"

"Actually, I'm on business. I'm helping detective Gomez gather information about the accident."

Looking surprised Laura said. "Why Charles, you didn't tell me you're a P. I., that's awesome." Then playfully, "You've been holding out on me."

"Oh, nothing like that. On occasion, when I was a professor, I used to help the Seattle Police Department."

She put down her grooming brush and said. "How interesting. How can I help?"

"I understand that Rusty was the only one to take care of Fury, did he take good care of him?"

"I suppose he did. I really don't know. I didn't go near Fury."

Charles said, "Did he ever take him on trail rides?"

"No, he used another horse. I did see him take Fury out for exercise. He took him out the other end of the barn."

"Do you have an opinion as to why Fury wasn't stabled in the other barn for boarding horses, it being more isolated?"

Looking quizzical, Laura answered, "Probably because Rusty spends more time in this barn." Laura picked up a comb and worked on Gallant's tail.

Charles put his notebook in his other hand, the one holding his pen, and patted Gallant on the rump. "What was the relationship between Rusty and Larry?"

"He had to keep him in line now and then.

'How so?"

"Larry would act stupid, he had a mean streak, and Rusty would put him in line."

"He knew about his taunting of Fury?"

"Yes."

"And he didn't let him go?"

"No."

Charles paused to write his notes and Laura continued grooming Gallant. "You were there during the Will, Larry incident, what did Rusty do?"

"He told Will to put down Larry and then they both walked into the barn."

"Was Rusty angry?"

"No, he was just stern. That's his nature. Quiet, rough around the edges."

"Did you ever see Will lose his temper? Other than the barn incident."

Laura paused her grooming and with the mentioning of Will her face softened. "No, Will has learned to cope with being the object of cruel jokes. He understood and handled it in a very controlled manner."

That was the Will Charles knew. "How about Larry's relationship with other employees?"

"He was arrogant. You know the type. I'm a college student, I'm just doing this temporary, and you guys have to do this the rest of your life. He wasn't well liked."

Charles thought, that matches Lisa's assessment. "Did he ever mention to you he needed the job to get through college?"

"No. I don't think he was trying to portray that image."

"What kind of car did he drive?"

"Late model sports car." Then Laura stopped grooming and turned to face Charles. Her face expressed sadness and fear. "I get the impression they found something that takes the focus off of Fury."

"It looks that way. I hope you won't talk to anyone about it.

"I won't."

"Who's the ranch veterinarian?"

"Brian McCarthy."

He thanked Laura and returned to his car, where he sat and looked at his notes. He knew it wasn't Fury but had nothing to eliminate Will as the primary suspect. He called Brian McCarthy. The veterinarian told him that Fury was not on any medication and didn't have any behavioral disorder. He was a broken spirited horse that was caused from his earlier mistreatment. He was surprised by the incident, but thought any horse may act violently if provoked.

Charles finished the lunch he picked up at the McDonalds, on the way to the University of Arizona, and parked his car in a parking garage.

He walked to the University Services Building, entered, and was greeted by a perky receptionist. Charles produced the identification card given him by Manny describing him as an auxiliary investigator for the Pima County Police Department and handed it to her. Holding it in her hand, her eyes went to the picture on the card and then to him, she decided it was a match.

Charles' past experiences with the card lead him to believe that most people don't really read the card. They see the Pima County Sheriffs Department's logo and look at the picture. Sliding the card back to him, she said, "What can I do for you?"

"I would like to get some information on a student, Larry Coleman." Charles said.

Her bubbly demeanor changed to somberness.

"Did you know him?" Charles asked.

"No, but everyone was talking about it. It's so sad."

"Do you know any of his classmates?" Charles asked.

"No," and then pointing to a bulletin board, "but Jason was, he organized a memorial service for him. Larry's body is being sent back to Indiana."

Charles walked over to the poster and read it as he wrote Jason Pittman in his notebook. He walked back to the receptionist and asked. "I would like to talk to the dean of admissions and the bursar. Are they available?"

"The dean is not available. I think the bursar is."

"I can get the information I need from a staff assistant. Is one available?"

"Yes I'll call ahead."

"Thank you. How do I get there?"

"The dean's office is down the hall, third one on the left, the bursar's is the last one on the right."

When he entered the dean's office, an elderly, gray haired lady with a stern look greeted him. She reminded him of a librarian whom Doris had worked with in Seattle.

"I understand you would like information on Larry Coleman, Mr. Knowles."

No preamble here, right to the point. "Yes, did he live on campus? Did he have any roommates? What were his activities on campus?" By having these answers, Charles thought he could get the names of his classmates.

"Let's use that table, it will be easier." Her eyes directed him to a table. "I'll go get his record."

Mrs. Ledbetter, which he learned from her nametag, sat quietly while Charles perused the record. Larry lived off campus in an apartment. He didn't participate in any campus activities, clubs, sports, or a fraternity. He wrote down the apartment address and the one in Indiana. At the latter lived his next of kin, his mother, Diana Coleman.

"Mrs. Ledbetter, are you familiar with the neighborhood that Larry's apartment was in?"

Looking at the address she replied, "Yes, a very nice area."

Charles needed a more descriptive answer than nice. "How would you rate it? Was it an average college student's apartment?"

"More than average. I'd expect a student from an affluent family to live in that area."

"Did you think he came from an affluent family?"

"Oh, I wouldn't know. Perhaps the bursar would know."

So, Charles left and headed to the Bursar's office. He stopped at an alcove that broke up the line of offices. It was furnished with a couch and two chairs. Oil paintings of the desert landscape hung on the walls.

He pulled out his cell phone and called Manny. "What's happening?"

"An illegal immigrant situation. The border patrol was chasing their van when it rolled over on I10. It's a mess. They're still counting the casualties. I10 west is shut down, but of more interest to you, the captain wanted an update on the Larry Coleman case. I went over it with him. He's very perceptive, and when he learned Will's a friend of yours, and saw that I was not in a rush for an arrest, he didn't push for one either. Although, he did asked if you came up with anything new."

"In a way I have. There are some things about Larry's life style that are contradictory. It may not have anything to do with his death, but I'm going to follow it up.

"Like what?" Manny asked.

"His finances. You can help me here. I don't want to call his mother at this time. It would confuse her and she would ask a lot of questions I can't answer. She lives in Franklin, Indiana. It's a small town and I thought you could call the department there and get some background information. Just verbal, no written report, I don't have much time, as you know." Charles felt fortunate to have Manny as a friend.

"I think I can do that," and then pausing, "it would be easier if I had a name and address."

"Diana Coleman, 376 Willow Street, Franklin, Indiana." Charles said.

Brandon Percival's secretary brought Charles into the office and made the introductions. He was a short man, gray hair, wearing a worn dark suit. "What can I do for you Mr. Knowles?"

Charles noticed that Larry Coleman's file folder was on his desk. "Did Larry have a scholarship?"

Brandon perused the folder and replied. "No, he paid the full out of state tuition."

"Did he have any outside scholarships?"

"There's no record of any outside reimbursement."

"Could you tell me what account the tuition checks were drawn from and who signed them?" Charles asked.

Brandon picked up the phone and said, "That wouldn't be in the folder. I'll have my secretary find out." As he waited for his secretary to find out, he said,

"What a violent way to go, so tragic, I understand he was kicked to death by a horse."

Wanting that scenario to last as long as it could, Charles said, "Yes, a very unusual way to go."

"This investigation of Larry's records, is that normal?" Brandon said.

"They like to know everything about the victim they can." Charles was relieved from further questions along those lines when the secretary came in with the information requested.

Brandon read the information in front of him. "Bank One, his account, his signature."

"Thanks, next I'd like to talk to some of his classmates. I have one named Jason Pittman. Do you know where I might find some others?"

"The Arizona Memorial Student Union. A lot of students hang out there this time of day."

Charles felt nostalgia as he walked through the main gate past old main and onto the mall. It was a long grass covered area separating a number of old and new university buildings. Palm trees were evenly spaced along the length of it. He walked into the student union through the open area with shops on each side and went down the stairs to the meeting room. He stood inside and saw all the study tables and computers actively being used. He realized it was folly to think he was just going to walk around and ask students if they knew Larry Coleman. He followed a group of students into a large open area full of study tables.

Charles sat at an empty table and opened his notebook. He looked at the information he got from the poster and decided to call the number that was under Jason Pittman's name.

It was answered. "Jason, this is Charles Knowles. I've heard about the memorial service and thought that it might be a good idea to post some flyers at the Trail Dust Stables. I think his friends there would like to attend. Do you have any I could bring back and post?"

"Yeah, but they're back in my room and I'm in the student union."

"What a coincidence, so am I." Charles stood up and viewed the room. "I think it's the study hall." He saw Jason stand up.

One of the students next to Jason moved so Charles could sit. Charles said, "Sorry about your friend. It was such a tragedy."

The students around Jason acknowledged this comment with, terrible, horrible, and gruesome.

Jason said, "Kicked to death by a horse. Crazy man, crazy. He was a cool dude."

"Yes he was well liked at the stables too. It shows a lot of character, working hard to put your self through college."

Two of the students across the table paused what they were doing and looked at Charles. Jason, with a– are we talking about the same person look– said, "Larry didn't have to work. He came from money."

One of the students who paused from reading said, "Yeah, his father died and left him and his mother well off."

The student next to him chimed in. "You should see his apartment and car."

"He worked there because he liked horses." Jason said.

During this interaction with the students, Charles noticed the student at the end of the table was very quiet, almost trance like, and when Charles did make eye contact with him, he adverted his attention. Charles, with his many years' experience as a professor, knew that look. He had seen it many times, dilated pupils, twitching, uncomfortable around people, especially strangers. This conversation made him very uncomfortable. The student took his backpack and moved to another table in the far corner.

Charles didn't want him to get away, so he told Jason that, with the information he got off his poster, he would have posters made back at the office.

Charles followed the anxious student to a vacant table and sat down across from him. "You seemed very uncomfortable back there, were you a close friend? What's your name?"

"Dan," and with a reluctant pause, "Taylor."

"In case you didn't get it, mine's Charles Knowles. Were you uncomfortable because you were a friend of Larry's or because a stranger was seeing you in your condition?"

"What are you talking about? Yeah, he was a friend. What condition?"

Charles leaned forward and looked Dan straight in the eye. I've spent a career dealing with students Dan and you're stoned. It's obvious."

"So what! What's it to you? What're you gonna do about it? Report me? Who the hell are you anyway?"

Charles leaned forward with his arms crossed on the table and said. "Relax. I'm not going to report you, but I must tell you to get counseling. I know you've been told that a hundred times, but it's not too late. As to who I am, I'm an investigator who's trying to gather all the facts I can to explain what happen to your friend. Was he a close friend, Dan? Did you hang out together?"

Dan settled down, now that the threat of exposure was gone. "Not really. What the hell. Shit it can't hurt him now." For the first time he focused his eyes on Charles. "He was my supplier."

Charles didn't show it, but he was taken back. This one statement explained the inconsistencies about Larry's financial status. Most murders are drug related. He felt the surge of renewed energy. Could it be possible this one was? "Just you?"

"No, a lot of students."

The mall activity had increased since his earlier crossing. He passed by a tent set up to sign up students for a credit card; the logic of signing up people who weren't employed escaped him. He answered his cell phone and was surprised to hear Manny so soon.

"Here's what I got." Manny said, "His mother lives in a modest home and works as a waitress. She has been divorced for about five years. Her husband was killed in a car accident. I think he needed that job at the stables."

"No he didn't, you see," Charles said, "he had an affluent apartment, sports car, and all his college bills were paid."

"All that from a part time job at the stables?"

Charles maneuvered himself across the bike lane and continued on to the garage. "No, from drug dealing on campus."

"Drug dealing. You're amazing. I can't believe that you came up with that kind of information so fast."

Charles agreed, "I can't either."

"It's good, but is it anything connected to his death?"

"I've no idea, but in a situation like this you just follow any information you have."

Manny's voice softened, "Everybody here, that's looked at the case, comes up with Will as the perpetrator. Even with this knew information, I don't think you can make a connection."

"Yes, there's a large gap there, but I think getting an answer to why he worked at the Trail dust might be the bridge. He certainly didn't do it for his love of horses, as one student suggested. We know that."

"It won't surprise me if you're a bridge builder too. I hope you're a fast one because I'll be case reviewing with the captain in the morning." Manny said.

Charles retrieved his car and headed back to the Inn. It was time for him to do some case reviewing too, and he knew that with Doris it would be much more productive and pleasant than with Manny's captain.

On his ride back to the Inn Charles called Doris and told her he would like to have dinner on their patio. Yes, he did have a lot to talk about and would review the day with her when he got back. The rest of the trip back, his thoughts were about Will. Did he have any idea he might be charged with murder in the morning? So far there wasn't anything to eliminate him as a suspect. He parked at the Inn and decided to check on Will before going back to his apartment.

Will's face brightened as he open the door and stood back as Charles entered. The room was warmly lit with an antique desk and floor lamp. Charles's attention was immediately drawn to a rocking chair with a cushion on the back and seat. "A new chair. Looks great."

Will answered, "Yes, it's very comfortable. Try it. Now we both have comfortable chairs to sit in." Saying this, he sat in an upholstered chair. "Lisa gave it to me. She's a very nice lady."

"Yes, she is. I see you added to your collection. Is that a pair of boots?" Charles got up and walked over to view this new addition. He picked them up and said. "They don't look worn enough to have been discarded, although they are stained. You going to wear them?"

"Can't, too small. Rusty has small feet."

"Rusty? Where did you find them?"

"At the Trail Dust, in the dumpster."

"When?"

"Yesterday morning. Would you like them? You have small feet, they might fit you."

Charles looked down at Will's feet and could understand why he thought everyone else's feet were small. "Thanks, I'll take them and try them on later."

"This is new too. It's a flashlight. Frank, the security man, gave it to me. He got a new one. It's got a holder to wear on your belt, just like a policeman."

"It looks like a powerful one." Charles said.

"Now, if I hear a hoot, I can go find an owl."

It occurred to Charles that Will was doing fine. He picked up the boots and headed to his apartment.

"Hi, I'm back. Boy that smells good." Charles closed the door and walked out on the patio where Doris was grilling shish-ka-bob. "I'm starving."

"You can sit down. This is almost ready." Doris lifted the grill cover and turned the ka-bobs.

The patio was their favorite spot and they spent many hours on it. When the renovation was done, two of the Inn's rooms were converted to an apartment. The existing patios were connected and made wider. Their apartment was on the second floor at the point where the wing connected to the main building, giving the patio an L shape.

Doris brought the meal to the table and said. "I saw you set something down. It looked like boots; did you get a new pair of boots?"

"Not really. It's a used pair of boots that Will gave me."

"I think Will takes recycling to a new level." Doris said.

Charles removed his ka-bobs from the stick. "In this case it may be a very important piece of evidence. It might be the first thing that takes the focus off of Will," he said.

"How so?"

"I'm not sure yet, but it does raise a lot of questions. Will found those boots in the dumpster Tuesday morning. He said they belong to Rusty and I noticed that they are stained. I'm going to have Manny check them out."

Doris glanced at the boots. "They don't look that worn. How did the rest of the day go? Did you interview everyone you wanted?" Doris cleared the table and brought their coffee with a plate of homemade cookies.

"I got some questions answered and some raised." As Charles said this, he opened his notebook. On one page of the small notebook he had written the questions for the interviewees with their answers. The opposing page he left blank for new questions and his comments.

Doris sipped her coffee. "Did you find out why Larry went back to the stall?" she asked.

"No but let me summarize the things I did find out. I found out Rusty lied in a statement to the police about Larry saying he needed the job to get through college. His student friends thought he came from money. He didn't. His mother was divorced and works as a waitress."

Doris couldn't wait for the end of the summary. "How could he possibly impress his friends with the idea he came from money on what he earned as a temporary worker at the stables?"

"That's it, he couldn't, but he could with the money he got from drug dealing. This, I found out from a friend who bought drugs from him."

With a look of astonishment, Doris said, "A drug dealer, working at the Trail Dust. You did have a productive day, but does it have a connection to his death?"

"I don't have a connection yet. What I have is a question as to why he worked at the Trail Dust. It doesn't make sense. It certainly wasn't a love for horses. Let me asked you a question. Who are drug dealers usually killed by?"

Doris moved closer to the table and rested her arms on the table. "Well, from what I read in the papers and hear on television," she said, "other people involved in drugs."

"That's it, certainly not by someone like Will, and Fury was not as bad as his reputation which was fostered by Rusty."

"Oh." Doris sat back in her chair. "Knowing Larry was cruel to Fury, why did Rusty keep him?"

"A good question. I think it would have to be for his benefit, but what that is I don't know."

"How did you learn that Fury wasn't as bad as his reputation?"

"I spent some time with him and talked to the veterinarian. It makes me think of someone putting up a sign beware of the dog to keep people from trespassing."

Doris got up and brought the coffee pot to the table. "I think you'll be on this awhile."

"That's for sure." Charles looked at his notes and verbalized some of the questions and facts. "Why did Larry go back to the stall? Was Rusty hiding something in the stall? Larry was killed in the stall adjacent to Fury's. His body was moved to Fury's." And then he looked at Doris and said, "The stall seems to be the focal point."

"How so?" Doris asked.

"I asked myself what was he doing there when he spooked Will? It was an empty stall. He wasn't working there. He was supposed to be checking the food and water in the stalls. That one was empty. Was he waiting for Will to work his way over next to Fury's stall? I don't think so. I think he was there to check out Fury's real temperament and then the opportunity to spook Will came up, giving him a reason for being there."

"You are in overdrive," Doris said.

"A good thing too, given the time frame I have for coming up with something. I also keep thinking about a detail that seems irrelevant."

With a curious expression, Doris asked, "What's that?"

"I've had a little experience with farms and animals and most use straw for the bedding of animals. They did at the Trail Dust and when Rusty came he changed to wood chips. One of the advantages of wood chips, and this was verified by Raul, is that they don't flatten down and move around like straw. Now focusing on the stall, this becomes another indicator of something being hidden there."

Doris stood up. "Charles, you have enough to keep you busy all night, but I have to get up early."

Charles got up and went to his desk. He switched on the desk lamp, placed his notebook on the desk, and sat down. He sat for a few moments, with his arms folded, he cleared his mind for a fresh assault on the information he had. He wanted to start at the beginning with the accumulated information to develop a new scenario. As he was scanning his notes, he realized he would have to inspect the crime scene again, particularly the stall. It was late, but that seemed to be the only thing he could do. It was late, but that might be a good thing, nobody would see him doing it and ask questions. Doris was sleeping, so he left a note on the refrigerator, picked up his flashlight, and quietly left the apartment.

It was a clear, warm night with the illumination of the full moon casting shadows along the dry riverbed path to the Trail Dust. It awakened all his senses, his adrenalin kicked in. He wondered, was it because of a primordial fear of darkness, or the sense of impending danger?

He moved the large barn door slowly until there was just enough space to get through. As he approached Fury's stall, he heard the horse stir and snort. He went to the adjacent stall and started to talk softly. "How you doing boy? Sorry to disturb your sleep. It's just your friend Charles." He put his flashlight in his pocket and used both hands to position himself on the stall partition. He reached in and patted Fury on the neck. Was this what Larry was doing, when he was looking for where Rusty hid his cache of drugs, and then when he realized he would be seen, needed a diversion.

Everything went the same as his first meeting with Fury. He left the adjacent stall and went into Fury's. Again, speaking softly, and making sure there was eye contact. When he reached the front of the stall, his attention turned to the floor. It was covered with a good layer of wood chips. He kicked the chips aside with his foot and thought he should have brought a rake with him, but he didn't and was very anxious to see if anything was under the wood chips.

After a few minutes, a line cutting the floorboards came into view. Charles dropped to the floor and using his hands brushed away the chips. He was very excited and said, "It's a hinged panel Fury, let's see what's under it." He put his finger in the hole of the panel and lifted it. Under the panel there was a space under the floor and in that space was a large metal box. On the lid of the box was a latch with a lock on one half of the latch. Charles took hold of the moveable part of the latch and lifted the lid. The box was empty, explaining the unused lock. Charles thought, what is it used for? The fact that drug dealing had surfaced in his investigation, drugs were the first things to come to mind.

Manny would have the box tested for any drug residue. He closed the lid and was about to put the panel down when he noticed a wire hung down where the hinges secured the panel to the floor. He leaned closer and could see the wire as it went toward the outside wall. He couldn't see where it met the outside wall, but in that position he looked toward the wall along the surface of the floor and saw the wire where it came up and went through to the outside.

Was it an alarm system? He got up and went outside to see if he could find out where the wire led. Then he realized if it was an alarm system, he had set it off. He would go back inside, hide, and see if anyone came to check the box. This thought faded with a flash of light, pain, and then darkness.

Was someone shaking him? Charles was bouncing on the back of a horse and very uncomfortable. He was slowly regaining consciousness. His head throbbed from the blow, and it being in an upside down position didn't help. He had a gag in his mouth and his hands were tied. Where was he going? Who did this? He turned his head and saw a brand-new cowboy boot in the stirrup. Now he knew. The horse left the dry riverbed and started up the canyon trail.

Will had returned to his room for the evening and was looking through his collection of marching band music. He made his selection and went over to place it in the tape player, but stopped short of putting it in. His head jerked and turned toward the window. Was that a hoot? He quickly opened the door and stood on the porch. A hoot. It was a hoot. Just like Charles said. He went inside, grabbed his flashlight, and scrambled down the path toward the sound. He stopped when he heard it again. Excited he aimed his flashlight at the top of a cottonwood tree. He froze in his tracks when he saw the big bright eyes of the owl staring back.

He had to tell Charles. Where was Charles? He switched off his flashlight put it in its holder and turned to go get Charles. In that moment he was startled by a large dark silhouette, it looked like a horse, moving down the middle of the riverbed and turning up the canyon trail. As he moved closer, he could see it was a horse with a rider and large bundle on the back. Drawn to it, he moved across the wash and followed it up the canyon trail. He was close to the horse when it reached a narrow switch back and stopped. This enabled Will to get close enough to see that the bundle on the back of the horse was a body.

Rusty stopped at this spot because of the sharp drop off to the canyon floor. It had a history of hikers having accidents, so it wouldn't be unusual to find Charles' body at the bottom. It had to look like an accident, so when Rusty lifted Charles off of the horse he laid him on the ground and untied his wrists. He took out his revolver and held Charles by the belt. "Get up. I know you're conscious."

The most piercing howl broke the night's silence. Both Charles and Rusty were dumbstruck at the sound and sight of a raging Will as he closed in on them. Charles fell back to the ground. Rusty raised his revolver waist high and fired. It hit Will, but nothing was to stop him in that rage. In the moment of contact, Rusty side stepped him and with both hands shoved Will, tumbling him to the ground. He raised his revolver and aimed at Will.

No one knew Rusty's last thoughts, but if they were there they would have seen Fury's rear end rise and two powerful legs propel Rusty into eternity.

Charles pulled the gag from his mouth and went over to Will. He knelt down next to him and said. "How you doing?"

Will bolted into a sitting position and said. "You all right?"

"I'm fine. You're the one got shot. Lay back down, so I can look at you."

Obeying Charles, Will stretched on the ground. The sight before him exhilarated an amazed Charles. The bullet had struck Will's flashlight. "You're going to be all right Will, but you'll need a new flashlight. Are you in any pain, Will?"

"I'm very sore."

"Let's get you to a doctor to be check out. Do you think you can get up on Fury?"

"Yes, that'll be fun, Laura's teaching me to ride. Fury is our friend, right Charles?"

"Yes, you saved me and he saved us."

Charles called Manny. He was used to being called late at night, but when he heard Charles' voice he became apprehensive. "I'm up on the Quail Canyon trail with Will. He's been shot. His flashlight took the impact. I'm bringing him down on horseback. Would you have the medics meet us?"

"Of course."

"And send a rescue team to the bottom of the canyon. Rusty is down there."

It was hard for Charles to believe it was only the next day. Following the doctor's advice, he was resting on a lounge on the patio. Doris had a scare, but refrained from scolding him for his foolishness, which she knew he couldn't help, and turned her energy into pampering him. "It's time for your medication." She handed it to him with a glass of water. "Why did Larry work at Trail Dust?"

"It was safer for picking up his drugs."

"So, he got greedy and tried to steal the drugs from Rusty." Doris sat down on a patio chair next to Charles."

"He realized the drugs were hidden somewhere in the barn and was clever enough to figure out Fury was being used as a junk yard dog."

"How did he possibly think he could get away with it? Wouldn't Rusty know?"

"Rusty dealt with a lot of people and there is a large amount of money involved. When Larry found out where it was hidden, he got very excited and didn't think it through. The alarm was attached to the floor panel not to the metal box. I did the same thing myself."

"I see a parallelism in the lives of Will and Fury. Both had problems when they were young, were defenseless, and were falsely suspected of violence." Doris said.

Charles, his thoughts returning to the canyon, said, "True, and both found the courage to act in the face of danger."

The door chimes interrupted them. Doris opened the door and saw Will. Doris said, "Hi Will, how you doing?"

"I'm black and blue, very sore. The doctor said I was very lucky and I'll be all right."

"Come in, Charles is on the patio. He will be glad to see you."

Will loomed over the reclining Charles. "You all right?"

"Yes, I'm going to be fine, I have to rest a day or two."

"And you?"

"I have to take Tylenol. I forgot to tell you I saw an owl last night. When you get better I'll show you where. It hooted just like you said."

Doris brought over another chair. "Sit down Will, you'll be more comfortable." She heard the chimes again and went to the door.

Charles thought listening to Will was stronger than the medication. It spread calmness throughout his body even his headache subsided.

Will continued, "Laura said I could take care of Fury."

Both looked up and greeted Manny as he followed Doris onto the patio.

Manny said, "You both look better than I expected. That was quite an ordeal you went through. And Charles, please don't do that again. That was dangerous. Call me, I've done the search."

Doris added another chair to the group. "We're having a patio party. Would anyone like a drink?" Hearing their affirmations, she went off to get a pitcher of tea.

Reaching into a bag he was carrying, Manny said. “These are for you Will, your watch and a new police flashlight and holder. The look in Will’s eyes told it all. It was like getting your first bicycle.

Charles asked Manny, “Did they find the murder weapon?”

“Yes, it was a shovel. Blood traces were picked up using Luminol.”

“How about Rusty?”

“His body was found at the body of the canyon. Not a pretty sight.”

Will looked up and said. “Truth be told, he was a very, very mean man.

THE END

NOW YOU SEE HIM NOW YOU DON'T

By A. C. Boyan

Charles and Doris Knowles were residents of the Iron Door Inn on the west side of the Catalina Mountains in Oro Valley, Arizona. At lunch, on the patio with Lisa Wright, the owner and manager of the Inn, Charles said, "Big crowd."

"We're booked full. It's the gem show. I love it," Lisa replied.

"I'm not sure how it's organized," Doris said, "is it one show or many?"

"Many," Lisa said. "It takes over the city. All the hotels and motels are booked."

"I saw huge tents set up west of downtown," Charles said. "It looked like a circus. I understand that some of them are only open to dealers."

"Some, and others are open to the public. Vendors come from all over the world."

"Excuse me, the tables all seem to be full, would you mind if I join you?" The interruption came from a portly middle age man with gray hair—bald on top, long on the sides—and a round fleshy face.

"Of course, we'd be glad to have your company. I'm Lisa Wright and this is Charles and Doris Knowles."

"I'm Fred Schumacher," he said, and extended his hand, "I overheard you talking about the gem show, that's what I'm here for."

"Are you a dealer?" Charles asked.

'No, collector. I've decided to sell my collection. I spent the morning showing it to vendors at the Arizona Pueblo Inn show." The waitress brought their lunch and took Fred's order.

"Did you have any luck?" Charles asked.

"No, but I have plenty of time left. Are you here for the show?"

"No, Doris and I are retirees. We came from Seattle and became residents of the Inn."

"With weather like this, I could move here in a minute. I'm from Milwaukee and when I get ready to retire, I'll certainly move to a warmer climate."

"What do you do there?" Doris said.

"I own a book store. It's been in the family for sixty years. My parents, German immigrants, started the business."

"Are there book chains in your area?" Charles asked. "I heard they are a problem for small book stores."

"They're affecting the small book stores." Fred took a drink of water. "It's tough to compete with them. I'm hoping to last until retirement. It's not just the money, I love working in the store.

"Is your collection valuable? Doris asked. "I've seen some people, near the downtown, with cases handcuffed to their wrist. Are you concerned about being robbed?"

"I use handcuffs on occasion. In order to get the insurance underwritten, you have to follow the guidelines given to you."

The waitress arrived with Fred's food. He thanked her.

Lisa asked, "Are you utilizing the Inn's safe?"

"Yes, that's one of the guidelines. I hired one of your security men, Jim Hightower, to accompany me when I'm moving with the case. I put it in the safe overnight."

"Excellent choice," Lisa said. "He's a fine young man. He's professional."

Charles placed his hands on the table. "Well, I have to excuse myself. I'm going gold panning, nice to meet you Fred."

"I've some specimens of gold in its natural state. Do you go often?"

Charles leaned back in his chair and said. "Will and I, he's an employee at the Inn, started about a month ago. We go hiking together and one day we met some people in the canyon doing it. Will got very excited about it and I found it interesting, so it was just an extension of our hiking."

"When I heard about it," Lisa said, "I thought it would be a great idea to include guests. We do limit it to six. That's all we have panning supplies for and it's just the right number for Charles and Will to comfortably handle.

"Sounds like fun. I was looking for an afternoon diversion from the show. Could I join you?"

"Do you have a spot open Charles?" Lisa said.

"No, but I could share my supplies with you, if that's all right with you?" Charles said.

"Thank you, that would be great. Where and when do I meet you?"

At one thirty, the small group gathered behind the Inn on the bank of a sandy river that had a small stream flowing in the center with mountain run off. The rain fall is seasonal and most of the year these river beds are dry. Under the shade of tall cottonwood trees, Will Smith stood next to Charles. Will was twenty six, broad shouldered—with a serious face that could turn into disarming smile. He was dressed in the garb of an old prospector, suspenders, pants tucked into his boots. The only thing missing was the pick.

Charles introduced himself and Will, and then led the group across the sandy riverbed, up an incline and onto a one-and-a-half-mile trail that led into the canyon. They took a side trail back down to the canyon floor. The river was flowing well. Further up the river, Charles heard the water cascade over large rock formations, but in this area, the terrain leveled off with the clear water running from bank to bank. Charles instructed the group on the technique used to pan gold and Will demonstrated it.

Fred went over to a spot described by Charles as having good potential for deposits. It was an area where rocks stuck out in the stream causing the flowing water to swirl and leave deposits of sand and gravel on the down river side of the outcroppings. Charles followed him.

A voice came from behind them. "Mind if I join you?" The man said, "My name is Tony Demarco. I got your name, Charles," and looked at Fred, "but I didn't get yours." Tony appeared to be in his early thirties.

"No problem." Fred extended his hand. "Fred Schumacher."

"I'm not sure I understood the procedure," Tony said.

Fred began to pan.

Charles said, "Here let me show you."

Tony waded into the water. "Wow, this is cold."

"That's one of the hardships you have to endure," Charles said.

They washed sand and gravel in their pans. The shade of the cottonwoods and rays of sun accented the water.

"That sounds like a Chicago accent," Fred said.

"Yeah, that's right. West side. Old Italian neighborhood. And you?"

Fred refilled his pan. "Milwaukee. My parents were German immigrants. You here for the show? You a dealer?"

"No, I'm just a tourist here to see the show and maybe pick up something I like." Tony got out of the water and stood next to Charles on the bank. "I guess I'm just a city boy."

"Too cold?" Charles asked.

"I don't spend much time in the outdoors," Tony said, "this is beautiful country; just the walk out here is beautiful. I don't know about standing in that water, but seeing people do this is fun. Do people ever find anything?"

"Not usually on these trips," Charles said, "it takes a lot of time and persistence to do serious gold panning. Most of the guests enjoy the scenery and the experience."

Will washed more pans than all of the other guests put together. Charles enjoyed watching Will with his eyes wide and fixed on the pan. That's why now he had a tinge of regret. "It's time to go Will. Did you find anything?"

"I have some black sand in my pan. Nothing under it though. Maybe next time."

"In the old days people could spend a lifetime looking for gold," Charles said.

On the way back Charles and Will were in the lead with the others, including Fred and Tony, behind them. At the end of the excursion, Fred and Tony approached Charles and suggested that they have dinner together, including Doris and Lisa. They could view Fred's collection, he said.

"That sounds great," Charles said, "I'll check with Doris and Lisa."

"Another fine evening on the Patio," Charles said, "I believe I've become spoiled. I expect it." The air was warm and the low sunlight spotlighted the west side of the mountains with pastel colors.

"Not to mention the fine food and service." Fred pushed his plate away.

"Thank you," Lisa said, "would anybody like dessert?"

"I'm anxious to see your collection Fred, is the invitation still open?" Tony said.

"Oh yes, let's go up to my room for the grand showing."

"It's in your room, not in the Inn safe?" Doris asked.

"For a short time, I use a portable security device," Fred reached into his pocket he pulled out a small device the size of a cell phone. "If any body enters the room this will go off."

When they got to the room, Fred went to the closet and took a case over to the bed and opened it. He opened the lock, removed three trays and placed them on the table. He took one tray at a time and removed each item from its wrapping and went on to identify it. He held up a diamond ring for them all to see, he said, "This is one of my favorites. It's an Edwardian diamond and garnet ring. My favorite period."

Doris whispered, "I have never seen anything so beautiful, that setting takes my breath away." The two women had leaned in, inches away, to observe it more closely.

"That's what makes it so special. It was part of my father's collection, which I inherited."

"I have no idea of the value," Tony said, "what would something like that be worth?"

Fred lowered his voice and said, "That's my most valuable piece. It's been appraised at $55,000 dollars."

A section of the lounge was set up around the brick fireplace for playing board games or cards.

Charles, after viewing the collection, sat with Will playing checkers. The bar, along the inside wall, had a few bar stools and tables. Playing checkers with Will could take some time, giving Charles time to observe the lounge activity. He looked over at the bar and saw Fred sitting on a stool. He was talking to a thirty-year-old woman wearing black slacks, and a colorful, southwest styled vest. He wondered if Fred mentioned having a wife. He couldn't recall.

"Your move Charles." Will said.

Charles made his move and Will double jumped him.

"Good one," Charles said. "You caught me sleeping."

While the waitress took Will's order for a Dr. Pepper and some popcorn, Charles looked over at two empty bar stools. They played two more games of checkers and switched to cards when they were interrupted by a scream.

Will bolted straight up out of his chair and pointed to the window with a view of the parking lot. "It came from out there." Charles and Will, along with other guests, rushed to the parking lot. When they arrived at the scene, a woman, the one who apparently screamed, stood over her companion who knelt over a man sprawled on the ground. Charles called 911.

Frank Boone, head of security, arrived and they both knelt down next to Jim.

"Where's the pain?" Charles asked.

"My left leg and arm. I tried to leap out of the way, but the corner of the car caught me."

Someone from the group that had gathered handed Frank a blanket which he placed on Jim. Charles elevated his feet and his head. A siren was heard in the distance.

"They'll be here in a minute Jim. Do think you can tell us what happened?" Frank said.

"I was getting off my shift and was walking to my car when I saw this lady moving fast to her car and opening the trunk. She was putting a steel banded black case into it. I thought it looked like Fred Schumacher's. I decided to check it out. Before I got there she backed out, and put it in drive and drove toward me. I don't think she ever saw me until the impact."

"Can you describe her?" Charles asked,

"She was wearing black slacks, a long sleeve, white blouse with a southwest styled vest, five six, slim build."

Charles and Frank stood up as the paramedics moved in to do there job. Charles tapped Frank on the shoulder. He nodded in the direction of the Inn. "Follow me."

They got no response when they banged on Fred's door. Frank opened it and they saw Fred gagged and handcuffed on the floor. They stood him up

The gag removed, Fred said, "They're my cuffs; the key is on the dresser." Frank removed the cuffs. "She stole my collection. I met her at the bar."

"Describe her." Frank said.

"Short blond hair, five six, thin, and she was wearing a white blouse with black slacks."

"Did she give you her name?" Charles said.

"Jennifer Fox."

"She was just seen putting your case in her trunk. After that, she ran over Jim Hightower."

"Is he all right?" Fred sat on the bed.

"Banged up, but he'll recover."

Detective Manny Gomez of the Pima County Sheriff's Department picked up his phone.

"Hi Charles, what's up?"

"We have a robbery here. Fred Schumacher. It was the women that committed the hit and run. I'll leave Frank to secure the room and I'll be with Fred in my apartment."

Before retiring to Arizona, Charles used his background in criminal psychology to help the Seattle Police Department. Shortly after his arrival in Arizona, Manny became aware of Charles' background while working on a homicide. They became friends and Manny consulted with him.

Charles put away his cell phone and addressed Fred, "I think it would be better if you and I went to my apartment, Frank can stay here to meet the robbery unit."

Doris brought coffee to the table and sat down. Charles explained, "I am an auxiliary member of the Pima County Sheriff's Department. I've worked on some investigations for them since we came out here. In Seattle, I was a criminal psychology professor and gave seminars on criminal behavior to their police department."

Doris said, "You must be heart broken? Some of those pieces were in your family for years. I know I would be."

"It's like losing a friend. And armed robbery, it was frightening." Fred rolled his eyes and raised his hands, palms opened.

Charles said, "You are insured, right?"

"Yes, of course."

The doorbell chimed. Doris introduced Lieutenant Detective Manny Gomez and Sergeant Steve Rodgers to Fred. The two of them sat down at the table.

"The robbery unit is already in your room," Manny said, "when they've done their job, they'll notify you when you can return. They'll also want a statement from you," then paused, "this is a delicate question, but I have to ask. What was the purpose of bringing this woman to your room?"

"To see my collection," Fred said.

Manny cleared his throat.

"She was a buyer," Fred said, "She had a shop. She said antique jewelry was her specialty."

Charles leaned back in his chair and ran his hand through his hair. It didn't make sense to Charles. "Did you think she was a possible buyer for the whole collection?" he said.

Beads of sweat were forming on Fred's forehead. "Maybe, you can't tell. She said she was very interested in antique jewelry."

Manny got up from the table and the rest followed suit. "Charles, I would appreciate any help you can give us, as usual, and Fred if you think of any thing that you think might help, give us a call, or tell Charles. We're trying to locate this Jennifer Fox right now. If we come up with anything I'll call you."

Vicky opened the motel door and said. "Shit, everything went wrong. Did I kill him?"

The visitor closed the door and moved into the room. "Where's the case?"

"Is that all you can think about?" Vicky picked up a drink and finished it in one gulp. "It's over there."

"We agreed, no alcohol, no drugs, no mess ups." The visitor's voice was low and scolding.

"I'm a wreck." She turned to fill her glass. She never did. A sharp crack from a low caliber gun at the back of her head was the last sound made in the room.

"It's Manny." Doris handed Charles the phone. Charles had just finished having breakfast on the patio, and now was sipping his coffee and reading the morning paper. "Morning Manny what's up?"

"We found her, or perhaps I should say the Pioneer Motel did. I'm there now. They found her body."

"Her body. How?" Charles said.

"Shot in the back of the head. The cleaning lady found her. Of course, we're not positive, but she does fit the description. Would you pick up Fred and come over for an ID?"

"Sure thing. That's on Oracle, right?"

"Right. Oh, another thing, the case is missing."

Charles put the phone away and explained the conversation to Doris. She said, "I wonder if Fred was more intimate with her than he admitted."

"A women's intuition."

"Last night, when he was here talking to Manny, I saw long brown strands of hair on his shoulder."

"I don't think it was that girl," Charles said, "She had short blond hair. I'm going to pick up Fred and take him to the Pioneer Motel for an ID. Maybe it won't be the same person."

Fred was visibly shaken when Charles gave him the information and was quiet on the trip to the motel, but when Manny showed him the body he actually started to tremble. Charles put on the latex gloves Manny handed him, and expected Fred to be sick at any moment.

"Yes, yes, that's her," Fred managed to force out the words, "my GOD, they killed her for the jewels."

"Why don't you wait in the lobby or car," Charles said, "I'll only be a few moments."

"Yes, I think I will." Fred quickly left the room.

The small room was busy with the forensic team gathering evidence. Charles went over to Manny who was standing next to the dresser going over Jennifer Fox's personal items in her shoulder bag. "Anything interesting?"

"Yes, but not surprising. Jennifer Fox just became Vicky Hobbs. How about you?"

"Nothing here. I was looking for an airline ticket," Charles said.

"I found it in the outside pocket of this bag. According to the ticket, she came from Milwaukee to Chicago to Tucson. Now we know a little about the victim," Manny said, "but what about the killer?"

Charles said, "He has professional experience and she knew the killer. There's been no forced entry. She allowed him to come up behind her, and there's no sign of a struggle."

"And we know the motive," Manny said, "a missing case loaded with jewelry. I'm going to notify the Milwaukee authorities to get a search warrant on her dwelling.

Both men took off their gloves and walked outside. Manny said, "I'll keep you informed as things develop."

"Same here." Charles replied as he headed to the lobby to pick up Fred.

Fred was the first to break the silence on the drive back to the Inn. "She stole my jewels and she was killed for them. I could have been killed. It's so terrible, such a young girl. Who could do something like that?"

Charles was sensing a feeling of guilt or fear coming from Fred that was stronger than he would have expected of him. Charles changed the. "The mountains are so beautiful. The one on the right is call Pusch Peak. It's named after a German immigrant."

Fred continued as if he didn't hear Charles. "I don't understand it. I take all the security precautions and I'm robbed and this Jennifer girl is dead. I feel guilty."

"It can happen. It was out of your control. The girl put herself in jeopardy. Her name was Vicky Hobbs."

Glancing over at Fred he saw his face was flushed and very tense.

"How do you know this? So soon."

"Manny looked at her license. I know this is silly but she was from Milwaukee, and it's a big place, but did you know her?"

"No, of course I didn't know her."

Charles pulled into the Inn parking lot. "Are you going to be all right?" he said.

"Yes, I'll be fine. I'm going to lie down."

Charles closed the door behind him. "I'm back."

"I'm on the patio."

Charles raised the table umbrella and sat down.

"Did you eat?"

"No. I didn't think it was a good idea. I thought Fred was going to be sick."

"I made some tuna salad. How does that sound? Let's have it on the Patio. Ice tea?"

"No, I think I'll have a beer."

Doris got the meal and drinks down and then sat across from Charles. "It would appear to me that you might have a lot to think about. How did it go?"

"It was the girl who robbed him."

"Live by the sword and die by the sword."

"In this case, a bullet to the back of the head. Fred was very upset." Charles poured his beer slowly into his glass.

"Understandable," Doris said nodding.

"Yes, but this goes beyond that." Charles took a drink of beer and sat back in his chair.

"How so?" Doris refilled her ice tea.

Charles reviewed Fred's behavior. "On the way back he said he felt guilt. He said if he hadn't shown her the collection, she wouldn't have been killed.

"Do you think he knew her?" Doris said.

"I'm not sure, but what bothers me is that I saw them in the lounge and the meeting just seemed too quick for Fred to invite her to see his collection."

"And," Doris said, "it would be too quick for a woman to decide to go to a strange man's room to see his collection."

"Exactly." Charles went to his desk and brought back his notebook. "Here's another, the showing of his collection to total strangers. What do you think?"

"He impressed me as being an out-going person. It could be his personality."

"Maybe he was setting up witnesses to verify the collection was in his room. Maybe he thought Tony, being a gem show enthusiast, would be able to authenticate the value."

"You think that he knew he was going to be robbed? Doris said, "Insurance fraud?"

"It's possible. He said it was armed robbery and no gun was found in Vicky's room." He wrote in his notebook. "After he showed us the collection, why didn't he put it in the safe? He told Lisa he usually did. Did he know he was going to show it again?"

Doris got up and cleared the table. "Insurance fraud that ended up with a murder. That's quite a stretch. I think those are all good question, but how are we going to find the answers?"

"Manny's already checking into Fred's background. I think I can help by making some local inquiries." Charles took out his cell phone and pressed the number.

After hearing Charles's questions and plan, Manny said, "Sounds like a plan

"I'm going to need to talk to the Brinks and insurance people. They'll probably want to verify my identification with you. And I want to check out Fred's flight information with Vicky's."

"Contact Don Anderson. He's in charge of security for the airport. I'll call and brief him about your visit.

"Good," Charles said, "anything new?"

"Vicky lived in the same neighborhood as Fred. They might have known each other. They're doing a search on her apartment right now."

"Interesting," Charles said, "I asked Fred about that and he said no."

Charles snapped his cell phone into its holder, and saw Doris hanging up the house phone. "That was Lisa," She said, " She's taking the afternoon off and wanted to know if I wanted to join her on a trip to the Outlet Mall. I assumed you would be busy the rest of the day, so I said yes." And then in a playful tone, "Unless you want to go too."

"Your assumption was right," Charles said, "I'll have to painfully pass on your offer."

Charles decided to start his inquiries with Jim. As he passed through the lounge, on the way to retrieve his car, he saw Fred in conversation with another man. The man's authoritative dress and manner made him think it might be about the robbery. He would check with Manny later.

He reached the second floor of the Northwest Hospital and was informed by the nurse in charge that he would have to wait a few minutes while Jim's vital signs were being checked. After hearing this, he decided to call Manny. "I'm at the hospital waiting to talk to Jim. On the way out of the Inn, I saw Fred talking to someone who gave me the impression he was on official business. Was it one of your men?"

"It wasn't one of ours, it was an insurance investigator." Manny said, "He was going to do a search of the room and asked if he could have a copy of the robbery units report on the contents of the room."

"I think I'd like to see that too."

"You will, Sgt. Rodgers is putting together a package for you. I called Don Anderson at the airport, he's expecting you."

"Thanks, I'm heading that way now." Charles replaced his cell phone and was informed by the nurse that he could visit Jim. The room was sunny and colorful with flowers on the windowsill. "How you doing?"

Jim smiled. "OK," he said, "luckily, just banged up. No breaks. I'll be released this afternoon."

"I didn't know you were such a popular guy." Charles went over and looked at the flowers and candy. To his comfort, Doris and Lisa had sent fresh flowers. Charles pulled a chair up next to the bed. "I got the OK from Manny to gather some information on the robbery. Could you go over your movements working with him?"

"Be glad to. Would you crank up the bed for me? Charles obliged with a few cranks of the handle. "After he checked in, that would be Monday evening. I went to the Brinks office with him and then returned to the Inn, where the case was put into the safe. The next morning, he called me and we got the case and went to a gem show at the Arizona Pueblo Inn."

"Do you know any of the vendors he spoke to?"

"One stands out. George Thornton, Thornton Jewels. We spent most of the time there." The nurse's aid came in to check his vital signs.

"That's a big help," Charles said, "glad you're doing OK. See you back at the Inn."

Charles headed for the airport. His interview with George Thornton, at the Arizona pueblo Inn Gem Show, verified his doubts that Fred was interested in selling his valuables. The statements he made about being at the gem show to sell his collection were false. George told him there was no reason for holding out to sell the whole collection. He said it was a very good collection and he was interested in buying some items. Fred said that if he didn't sell it by the end of the show, he would come back later.

With the number of security people on duty at the Tucson International Airport, it wasn't hard to locate Don Anderson's office. The office had modern style furniture and two big windows overlooking the runways. Underneath the windows was a credenza with a picture of his family, Charles assumed, and a model of a Boeing 747 jumbo jet. The in and out file trays were full, but the rest of the desk was neat. A set of papers was spread out in front of Don.

"I got a copy of Vicky's and Fred's airline tickets for you," Don said, "Manny also mentioned you may have some other questions." Don slid the copies over for Charles to peruse.

"They both flew on the same flight," Charles said, "although they sat in different sections. Very interesting, and Fred's ticket is one way. Can I get the information about Fred's checked baggage?"

Don smiled. "Yes, you can. It's on the second page."

Charles read the information on the second page which revealed one at 25 lbs. and the other at 15 lbs., then asked. "What are the weight limitations on checked baggage?"

"Most of the airlines allow two pieces of luggage with a maximum of fifty pounds each. They charge an additional fee for anything over that."

Charles put copies in his notebook. "Thanks, Don, you've been very helpful."

Don stood up. "Nice meeting you. If you come up with any other questions, just give me a call."

The next and last stop was the Brink's office. A chain link fence topped with coiled razor wire surrounded the near windowless building. Seeing the formidable trucks parked at the side of the building and thinking about the large sums of money and valuables they transported always gave Charles a feeling of intrigue. He was informed the manager was Ted Harris and was lead to his office. Ted was in his mid-forties and graying at the temples. His eyes were deep set in his round, ruddy face. After some preliminary banter, which included his mentioning Manny's call, he sat upright facing Charles across the desk waiting for his questions.

"What kind of contract did Fred have with you?"

Perusing a paper in front of him, Ted said, "The valuables were to be picked up at his book store in Milwaukee and delivered to the Tucson office where he was to accept delivery."

"Is there anything unusual about that?" Charles asked, "I'm not familiar with the business."

"Some people do it, but we advise against it. We have a trade fair service that will pick up the goods from an office and deliver them to a show site on a pre–arranged date and time. On the closing day of the show we'll pick up the goods at the show and return them to the office. We always recommend you don't carry your valuables around with you. "What about insurance coverage?"

"It was insured for $600 thousand while in our possession."

"How about while he was staying at the Inn?" Charles said.

"That would be covered under his business insurance."

Behind Ted, were pictures on the wall showing some of the most valuable items Brink's had transported in the past. "Who did that bat belong to?" Charles asked.

Ted was only too glad to share some of Brink's history. "That was Hank Aaron's." Ted said. "The one used to break Babe Ruth's home —run record."

"Did Fred have a return contract for his valuables?" Charles asked.

"No."

"No."

"That wouldn't be necessary. He would just bring them back for shipment."

"Thanks," Charles said, "I appreciate your time."

Ted stood up and extended his hand. "No problem."

Charles glanced at his watch. It would take him about forty minutes to get back to the Inn. At the next red light, he took out his cell phone, and called Manny. "I'd like to go over things with you. Do you want to stop by on the way home? We could have dinner at the Inn."

Manny said," I've got family commitments tonight, but I can come over about eight thirty."

"Sounds good."

When Charles pulled into his parking space on the side of the Inn, Will was returning to his room in the maintenance building. A broad smile crossed Charles' face. Will was carrying something back to his room. Will was a scavenger. One of his jobs was taking the trash out to the dumpster, but if it looked like it could be used, he added it to his collection. Some of the things he would keep and others he gave away. Charles didn't want to take the time now to view this new acquisition, but he would inquire about it later.

Charles walked into their apartment and saw Doris with her new dress on twirling in front of a full length mirror. "That looks great," he said.

"I saved sixty dollars. It was marked eighty and I paid twenty. I love it." Doris turned her back to the mirror and looked over her shoulder. "It fits perfect. Are you hungry? Lisa and I had a late lunch. Want me to fix you a sandwich?"

"That would be fine." Charles said.

Doris put away her purchases and said. "How did you do?"

"I met with everyone I wanted to and picked up some interesting information that I'm going to discuss with Manny. He's coming over at eight thirty."

"For dinner?"

"No. I asked him, but he had other commitments."

"Oh, Sgt. Rodgers dropped off that package for you. I put it on your desk."

"Good, I'll look at it while I am having my sandwich."

The phone rang and Doris answered it. "Hi. Oh I love it. I just took it off. It was fun. Really? That's interesting. I'll tell him."

Charles sat at the patio table and opened the package. The pictures of Fred's room showed only one suitcase.

Doris returned to the patio and said, "That was Lisa. She said that when she came back, one of the maids told her that while she was cleaning Fred's room, a man came in and looked all around the room. He said he was just checking to see if all the rooms were the same."

"Could she describe him?" Charles asked.

"Yes. From the description, it was Tony Demarco. What do you think he was looking for?"

Charles added this to his notes. "He probably suspects insurance fraud and thought Fred still has the jewels some where."

"But they were stolen by that girl and she was murdered for them." Doris said.

"Which raises a very key question, why does he still think that Fred has the jewels?"

After leaving Fred's room, earlier that day, Tony went to the lounge and sat at the end of bar facing the entrance to the Inn. What else could he do? He didn't see it in the room. It could have been in one of the draws, but he wasn't about to go through the draws with the maid there. At the time, he had been sitting at the same place at the bar. After viewing the jewels with the others, he witnessed the two of them going up to the room and saw Vicky when she left with the case. Fred was clever, he made a switch, but at some time he had to take those jewels back with him. Yes, Fred would lead him to the jewels. Just then he spotted Fred coming through the door.

At precisely eight thirty, Doris answered the door chimes and took Manny out to the patio. He placed his notebook on the table and sat across from Charles. He said, "I see you've gathered some information. Any theories?"

"Yes, I have. At this point though, it's only on the robbery. I believe Fred was responsible for the crime with the help of Vicky Hobbs."

Doris brought coffee and brownies and sat down at the table. "The fact they came in on the same plane and, after a quick meeting in the lounge she went up to his room, is too much of a coincidence," she said.

"True, and also a general review of his statements and reactions just don't add up to normal behavior. Another thing I suspected, and later verified by George Thornton, was that he could have sold off the jewels individually."

"Was there a financial gain by selling it as a collection," Manny asked.

"No. The Brink's manager told me he didn't have a return contract, but I've been told that might not be that unusual. The thing I did find unusual is he bought a one way plane ticket."

"How was he planning to go back?" Doris asked.

Charles leaned back in his chair and ran his hand through his hair. "I think that he didn't want to carry the jewels with him on the plane. Too risky. I think he may have planned to drive back."

"Manny said, "I'll have Sergeant Rodgers check his car rental contract. The information we've developed proves we're on the right track. The Milwaukee Police did a search of Vicky's room and found out she was employed at the bookstore. Two of the employees of the store were interviewed and identified her picture. They didn't think any additional help was necessary. When they asked Fred about it, he said that it was only temporary and he was trying to give her a new start, from what the employees didn't know, but suspected is she had a drug problem. So, I think that proves your theory."

Charles said, "If that solves the insurance fraud question, it leaves us with the bigger problem of solving a murder."

"That accident in the parking lot seems to have thrown a monkey wrench in somebody's plan," Doris said.

"It's possible that when Vicky ran over Jim, Fred feared exposure and killed Vicky?" Charles poured himself another coffee.

Manny got up and walked over to the patio rail. He looked up at the clear night sky and stretched.

Charles sipped his coffee. Manny returned to his chair and said. "Now I have to add more complications to our mystery. What if Fred enlisted Vicky for his insurance fraud plan, but Vicky had already been recruited in a plot to steal Fred's collection?"

"Manny what makes me think you have information to back up that if."

"Because I do. The police found a log in her room. In it she wrote down Fred's movements while she was working in the store. Her accomplice wanted to know where Fred kept the jewels and on what occasion he might take them out."

"Did she mention her accomplice?"

"In the log she notes that Joey is going to like this. These are the times she actually saw the Jewels. A couple of times she saw a middle age woman looking at them."

Doris set down some of Charles' notes, and said, "Was he married, or did he have a girl friend?"

"Not that we know of.

"It must have been after this that Fred recruited Vicky for his plan," Charles said.

"When Joey heard that, he must have been happy. All he had to do is let Vicky go through with Fred's plan and then they would double cross him."

Charles asked, "What's your next step?"

Manny lowered his cup of coffee and said, "I've asked the Milwaukee Police to identify Joey for me. There might be some prints in Vicky's apartment. A picture of this Joey would be a big help."

Charles gathered his notes. "I don't think Fred should be questioned at this point," he said, "it might spook him. I'm going to watch him carefully and maybe get some information from casual conservation. I'm very curious about how he plans to return to Milwaukee."

"Sounds like a plan," Manny said.

Both men stood up and walked to the door. At the door, Charles said, "I've an idea. If I walk you out, maybe by chance we would run into Fred in the lounge."

Manny nodded, "That would work."

Charles turned toward the kitchen and said, "I'm going to walk Manny to his car."

"Why?" Doris said, "Is he afraid of the dark?"

Will was coming back from the Trail Dust Stables where he spent his off hours from working at the Inn. He loved horses and was being taught to ride. When he reached the parking lot, he saw Charles and Manny in front of the Inn.

He quickened his pace and shouted, "Hi Charles, hi Manny."

"Hi Will." Charles called.

"Looks like he's coming from the Trail Dust." Manny said, and when Will approached them he added, "Good to see you, Will. Learn to ride yet?"

Will broke out in a wide grin. "Yes, I have. Laura's a good teacher. Next week I'm going on a trail ride."

"I saw you earlier," Charles said. "It looked like you added to your collection."

"Yes I have," Will said, "Now I can put some of my collection in it. It's broken, but I can still use it."

"What is it?" Charles asked.

"OH, it's a case. It's very strong. It has metal edges around it.

Charles and Manny looked at each other.

Charles asked. "Could we see the case?"

When they reached Will's room, the case was next to the bookcase that held Will's treasures; an old clock, flower pot, picture frames, and rocks.

Manny reached into his pocket and pulled out two pairs of latex gloves. He gave a pair to Charles—they examined the case.

"Will, this case may be evidence in a crime," Charles said. "Do you mind if we take it? We'll replace it with a new one."

"OK."

At the car, Manny placed the case on the back seat.

"The prints should tell us if it's Fred's." Manny said, "I feel confident that it is, too much of a coincidence, but if it was Fred that put it in the dumpster, it will connect him to the murder."

"I don't think it was."

"No?"

"If it was Fred, he wouldn't have had to break the lock."

"Maybe when they take the prints off of it," Manny said, "we'll get a better idea who handled it. I'll send a lab man over to take Will's prints. You want to be there?"

"Sure, have him call when he comes to take them."

"Let's assume for a moment that it wasn't Fred that threw it in the dumpster," Manny said, "this would suggest the perpetrator is staying at the Inn."

"Which brings in our third character in the robbery plot," Charles said, "the mysterious Joey."

Manny put one hand on the steering wheel and the other one, holding the keys, in the ignition.

Charles opened the door and then said. "I got a feeling those jewels are on the property. I'm going to get up early and keep an eye on Fred, or anybody else who's keeping an eye on him."

"Sounds like a plan." Manny said.

Charles leaned in and said, "If Fred didn't trust Vicky and gave her an empty case, whoever murdered Vicky also got an empty case."

"And maybe looking for the jewels."

"Which gives us another problem," Manny said, "We were there when Fred was handcuffed on the floor and right after that the robbery team searched the room. They didn't find any jewels."

"The photos show one suitcase in the room," Charles said, "I remember seeing two. The information I received at the airport shows he checked two bags. The combined weight of both bags could have been carried in one. Maybe he made a switch.. I saw the jewels in his room and then saw Fred in the lounge. It could be in that time lapse that he moved them."

At exactly six thirty Thursday morning Charles sat enjoying his complimentary breakfast in the lounge. He chose his spot for its view of the lobby area and the front entrance

Last night, when he reviewed the case with Doris, it was clear to him that in Fred's insurance fraud plan he needed Vicky, but because of her drug problem, he didn't trust her with the jewels. The Joey character didn't plan on that and would be looking for the jewels.

Guests slowly filled up the lounge. He looked up and saw Tony Demarco carrying his food to a table near the front entrance. He turned his head and saw Fred pulling his suitcase and stopping at the front desk.

Charles slightly lowered his newspaper so he could watch both men. He felt the excitement surge through his body. Fred was checking out, but with only one bag. Charles would wait for the right moment to follow him.

To Charles's surprise, Fred, when he reached the door, turned left and went down the aisle, between the lounge and the front wall, leading to the restrooms. Charles shifted his position in his chair to get a better view of that area. He noticed that Tony looked in that direction.

He sipped his coffee, raised his newspaper and waited, and waited. Too much time had passed for someone to use the restroom. He sensed something was wrong. He looked over at Tony's table. He was gone. What went wrong? And then thought, I didn't see anybody leaving the restroom, but wait, I did—a heavyset woman with shoulder length, brown hair. Suddenly those bits of information, so meaningless standing alone, connected to give him the answer he was looking for. He headed for the front door with a hand on his cell phone.

By the time he reached his car, he was talking to Manny. "Fred checked out. I'm trying to follow them, but they got a head start on me."

"Where are you now?"

"I'm turning on to Oracle. I don't see them ahead." Charles accelerated. "I hope you'll take care of any tickets I get."

"No problem. I'm leaving with Sgt. Rodgers.

Did you see them?" Manny asked.

"Yes. I wasn't the only one staking out the lounge. Tony Demarco was there and he didn't fall for the switch." Charles weaved between the cars. "Maybe this commuter traffic will slow them down."

"The switch?" Manny asked.

"Yes, Fred changed into a matronly looking woman. But he was only carrying one bag. The paisley bag with the jewels in it must be stashed somewhere. That must be how he moved the case out before the robbery." Charles slowed down, the traffic was mounting.

"Charles be careful and take it easy. Sgt. Rodgers learned that Fred rented his car from Enterprise on First and Oracle. We'll meet you there. He will have them give him a ride to wherever he going."

Charles let out a sigh of relief. "That makes sense."

As Charles approached the Calle Concordia intersection, he saw the flashing lights of the patrol car as it entered the intersection and turned right. The patrol car slowed down and Charles pulled up behind the patrol car. Five minutes later both vehicles pulled into Enterprise Car Rental. Inside they learned that the car was turned in by a woman who matched the description of the woman Charles saw leaving the restroom at the Inn. They learned from the trip log that she was being given a courtesy ride to the Greyhound bus station. Charles asked if anyone noticed how many bags she was carrying and the clerk, who had observed her in the lobby waiting for her ride, said that she had only one.

The three of them sat in back of the patrol car and headed for the Greyhound bus station, Charles said, as though answering his own question, "A locker in a bus station would be a good place to leave the jewels until you were leaving."

Manny turned in the front seat and faced Charles. "I hope we get to him before Joey. We got information that the Joey mentioned in Vicky's log is Joey Lorenzo. They sent his picture and prints. Not only is it a picture of Tony, but also the prints match a set taken off the case found in the dumpster. He's a career criminal and I believe he killed Vicky. I hope we get to Fred and the jewels before he does." Manny turned and faced the front again and spoke to Sgt. Rodgers. "Make a call to have some back up meet us outside the Greyhound bus station. Tell them to keep a low profile."

The courtesy van pulled into the bus station parking lot. The driver got out and retrieved Fred's suitcase. Fred tipped the driver and snapped the handle of the suitcase in the up position.

He then walked into the bus station and, from a locker, retrieved the paisley suitcase carrying the jewels. He left the bus station, turned left, crossed Congress Street, and went into the Congress Street Hotel.

Inside the hotel he turned and looked out the window. He took a handkerchief from his purse and wiped his brow. Ordinary people walked by the hotel and some walked in. His eyes followed each one. After about five minutes, he adjusted the purse strap on his shoulder, took the handles of the suitcases, and walked through the lobby. This entrance, on the opposite side of the one he came in, exited into a parking lot. He paused again and scanned the area.

Sgt. Rodgers pulled up in front of the bus station and stopped. At the same time, two-motorcycle policemen pulled into the parking lot across the street and positioned themselves facing the bus station. Manny nodded in their direction and said. "Sergeant, make contact with them."

Inside the bus station, Charles and Manny scanned the area. To the left of them, two lines were formed at the ticket counter. In front of them, wooden benches filled the lobby. The far wall had glass doors and windows, separating the lobby from the loading platform. One of the busses was being loaded.

To the right of the lobby was a passageway that led to the restrooms, and to the right of this there were rental lockers of different sizes that filled the wall. Fred was nowhere in sight.

Manny said, “I’ll check the bus.”

“I’ll check the restrooms and the cafe,” Charles replied.

Fred wasn’t in the café. Charles checked the men’s room. Nothing. It had to be the ladies room. He walked back out to the lobby and asked a lady if she would check the ladies room for him. He told her the bus was getting ready to leave and he couldn’t find his wife. In a few minutes she came back with a negative reply.

Two men returned outside and stood in front of the glass doors.

“It doesn’t seem possible that we lost him,” Manny said, “I’ll have to check Enterprise to make sure this is where they dropped him.”

A taxi stand was on a small street next to the parking lot. In it, four cabs waited in line for the next fare. Two cabbies waited outside their cabs sitting in aluminum fold up chairs. Two others stood next to them talking. Charles said to Manny, “I’ll be right back.”

“Morning.” Charles said to the cabbies.

The older man, who was sitting, got up. “You need a cab?”

“No, I wondered if you saw an older woman with shoulder length brown hair, wearing a tweed jacket and dark brown pants. She was dropped off by an Enterprise van.”

“Did she go in the bus station?” Charles said.

The man sat back in his chair and said. “Yes.”

He handed the man five dollars and turned to leave.

The man thanked him and said. "But she came out."

"Did she take a cab?"

"No," he said, "She just walked to Congress Street." The man pointed in the direction of the Congress Street hotel.

Charles thanked the man again, crossed the driveway, and motioned to Manny who was watching him. He told Manny what the cabbie said. They faced the Congress Street Hotel and a little further away the newly restored Southern Pacific Railroad.

"You think he went to the hotel?" Manny asked.
"No, I don't," Charles, said, "I think he went to the railroad station. This was just part of his diversion."

Manny signaled to Sergeant Rodgers who then pulled the cruiser up next to them. They got in and Manny said, "The railroad station."

Fred entered the station and turned left. This led to the restrooms, baggage check in, and the Amtrak ticket counter. He followed the passageway that led straight and ended at the lady's room. Just before the lady's room he turned right into a small corridor that led to the men's room and waited outside. After a few minutes, he went in. The stalls were made of stainless steel and the floor was tiled. He pulled his suitcases into the handicapped stall and bolted the door. Opening his suitcase, he took out men's clothes.

Tony entered the station through the same entrance as Fred, but once inside he walked over to the counter and picked up a train schedule. He held the schedule in front of his face and looked over the top of it into the passenger waiting area. He scanned the long, back-to-back, wooden benches. Fred wasn't there. Tony turned and viewed the Amtrak ticket counter. Not there either. The restroom sign was clearly visible above the passageway. Tony paused where the corridor of the men's room met the passageway. He looked at the lady's room and then went into the men's room. No one else was in there. When he looked under the space between the stall door and the floor he saw the bottom of a suitcase under the handicapped stall. The fabric pattern was a colorful paisley. Tony took a Leatherman micra pocket knife from his pocket and opened the screwdriver blade. With his right hand, he took a Griptilian knife from his jacket pocket and with the rotation of his thumb unleashed a three-and-a-half-inch blade. He positioned himself in front of the stall. He inserted the screwdriver blade into the lock mechanism under the door handle and with a counterclockwise motion released the bolt.

The door swung out and exposed Fred with his back to the door in the process of changing his clothes. Tony's left arm, the one that held the Leatherman, went around Fred's neck. He used his knee for support, arched him back and drove the knife blade into the small of his back. Fred collapsed on the floor. Tony cleaned the blade in the toilet bowl and then flushed the toilet. He wiped the blade on Fred's shirt and returned it to his jacket pocket. He took the paisley suitcase, bolted the stall door, and left the men's room.

Sergeant Rodgers stopped the cruiser at the entrance to the railroad station. The two motorcycle policemen pulled up next to them on the road and waited for instructions. Manny opened his door and said. "Isn't that Tony in front of us?"

Charles got out of the back of the cruiser. "That's Tony, and he's pulling the bag."

Manny pointed to him and signaled the motorcycle policemen to move. He then shouted orders for Tony to stop. Tony turned and saw the two motorcycle policemen dismounted and approaching him. He withdrew his gun and fired, hitting both policemen.

Both shots from the low caliber automatic, although accurate, were ineffective. One officer was hit in his bulletproof vest and the other in his helmet, but it didn't stop the policemen from returning fire. Manny and Sergeant Rodgers also fired at the same time.

Charles watched from the cover of the front of the police cruiser and saw Tony's body slam into his car and slump to the ground. The four policemen stopped firing and moved cautiously toward the body. Charles followed the group and watched as the body was checked for signs of life. In the distance, sirens could be heard. While Manny issued instructions, Charles thought about Fred. Where was Fred? He turned and ran to the train station.

Inside the station, people had lined up at the windows when they heard the commotion outside. Inside the door the security guard watched the action in the parking lot. Charles saw him and motioned to him to follow him. Having seen Charles with the police outside, the security guard acted immediately and followed Charles as he walked and scanned the passengers. Not seeing him in the open area of the station, he rushed to the restroom. When the security guard opened the handicapped stall, they saw Fred's body sprawled on the floor. Charles returned outside and notified Manny that Fred's body was in the men's room. He then gave his statement to the police officer recording them from witnesses and went to the bus station to take a cab back to his car.

When Charles entered the apartment, he called to Doris. "Doris, I'm home." He then went to the refrigerator and got an ice tea that he brought out to the patio and sat down.

Doris came out of the laundry room and followed him onto the patio. "You've been gone a long time; did Fred lead you to anything?"

Charles nodded his head and made a deep sigh. "Did he ever", he said. And then went on to describe the events of the morning.

With a look of disbelief Doris sat down at the table. "Fred is dead? Killed by Tony? Fred seemed like such a nice man. Women's clothes? The whole thing seems extraordinary."

"Oh, that it is. Fred got greedy. He wanted to keep his collection and save his business. That in itself would fall into the common insurance fraud scheme, but what I find truly amazing is the fact that it enhanced a plot already in place by a ruthless killer."

"That's another thing. Tony—a killer? He was right here among us. We had dinner with him. It gives me chills to think about it." Doris shook her head and shoulders.

"Thanks to your keen sense of observation, that strand of hair on Fred's shoulder, and putting that together with the feminine suitcase, I was able to follow him this morning." Charles said affectionately.

"But it didn't save Fred," Doris said.

"No, but it did take a killer off the streets."

THE END

www.ingramcontent.com/pod-product-compliance
Lightning Source LLC
LaVergne TN
LVHW020636100826
845148LV00012B/2200

9780967179513